W9-CQU-023

In Big Trouble

"Congratulations," Ms. Crowley said. "The four of you are the new members of this year's Yearbook Committee."

"There must be some mistake," Heather managed.

"There's no mistake. You will be writing tag lines for every member of the graduating class."

"What's that supposed to mean?" Ashley mumbled.

"It means 'Most Likely to Succeed,' 'Cutest Couple,' 'Most Popular.' . . ."

" 'Most Likely to Be Followed and Tortured Horribly,' " Terry volunteered.

Ms. Crowley's mouth was set in a thin little line. She looked like she was enjoying herself. "The four of you are the most unmotivated, most uncooperative individuals I've seen in a long time. Every one of you has some kind of attitude problem, and I'm telling you right now that if you don't shape up, you're going to be in big trouble. . . .

**Other Point paperbacks
you will enjoy:**

Changing Places
  by Susan Smith

Hello . . . Wrong Number
  by Marilyn Sachs

High School Reunion
  by Carol Stanley

Misjudged
  by Jeanette Mines

Saturday Night
  by Caroline B. Cooney

The Bet
  by Ann Reit

point

YEARBOOK

Melissa Davis

SCHOLASTIC INC.
New York Toronto London Auckland Sydney

Scholastic Books are available at special discounts for quantity purchases for use as premiums, promotional items, retail sales through specialty market outlets, etc. For details contact: Special Sales Manager, Scholastic Inc., 730 Broadway, New York, NY 10003.

No part of this publication may be reproduced in whole or in part, or stored in a retrieval system, or transmitted in any form or by any means, electronic, mechanical, photocopying, recording, or otherwise, without written permission of the publisher. For information regarding permission, write to Scholastic Inc., 730 Broadway, New York, NY 10003.

ISBN 0-590-40205-6

Copyright © 1987 by Betty Anne Crawford. All rights reserved. Published by Scholastic Inc. POINT is a trademark of Scholastic Inc.

12 11 10 9 8 7 6 5 4 3 2 1   7 8 9/8 0 1 2/9

Printed in the U.S.A.   01

First Scholastic printing, May 1987

1

The weak spring sun slanted obliquely through the long, narrow windows of Prescott High's Room 220. The four of them sat in the empty classroom after school, trying to sneak looks at one another without getting caught. Finally Ashley DeWitt, least likely to care about what other people thought about her (at least on a grand scale), sighed tragically, folded her arms across her desk, and buried her face in the crook of her elbow. Ashley's wild, dark, curly hair spread across the back of her cotton Fair Isle sweater, handknit in the same colors as the flowers printed on her skirt. She wore charcoal-gray tights, red ankle socks, and short black boots.

Across the room, Heather Mercer pulled her shoulder bag onto her lap and took out a mirror. The mirror was shaped like human lips. Heather dug around in her purse until she came up with a lipstick. She began applying Heartbreak Red to her mouth with a small brush, staring in the mirror at her perfect face surrounded by blonde hair. Anyone could see that Heather Mercer was doing more than just putting on lipstick. She was performing an act of love. Heather Mercer was the most beautiful girl in Prescott High School, and she felt that her life was full of responsibility because of that.

Terry Wallace sat in the last seat of Heather's row directly in front of a poster that showed the basic muscle groups of the human body. The muscles were mostly red with strips of blue and yellow, all banded together with what looked like white adhesive tape.

Terry wasn't looking at the poster. He was picking through the pockets of his vintage forties vest, hunting for the button that had fallen off his red suspenders. Terry tossed his long, straight reddish-blond hair out of his eyes and caught Heather Mercer staring at him in her mirror. Terry winked. Heather frowned. Terry looked over at Ashley, but Ashley was hopeless; she was in two of his morning classes, and she didn't live in the real world. She was interplanetoid. Like right now there she was, not looking at anything but her desk. Close up.

Meanwhile, Blaze Conrad slumped against the teacher's desk at the front of the room, his hands jammed into the pockets of his leather jacket, his black motorcycle boots tapping out an imaginary drum solo made up entirely as he went along. Blaze's dark eyes were watching Terry watch Ashley and Heather. Blaze was dressed totally in black: black jeans, black T-shirt, black leather jacket. Black and silver were Blaze's favorite colors.

Heather lowered her mirror and stared pointedly at Blaze's feet. "You're taking this whole thing really seriously, huh?"

Blaze shot Heather a chilly glance. "At least I'm not slopping petroleum products all over my face."

Heather snapped her mirror shut and turned around to stare at Terry. "Does anybody know what we're all supposed to be doing here?"

Terry gazed warmly and devotedly at Heather. "Can I be your slave forever?"

Heather didn't answer.

Blaze sat on top of the nearest desk and tucked his hands under his thighs. "We're waiting for Ms. Crowley, what else. We're Crowley's Captives."

"Anybody know what she wants?" Heather asked.

"Way I see it," Blaze drummed his fingers on his knees, "she'll tell us when she gets here."

"Aren't you worried?" Heather insisted. "Maybe this is serious or something."

"Yeah, I can tell you think it's serious." Blaze was sarcastic.

"Aw, come on, okay?" Terry complained. "Leave her alone."

"I'm not doing a thing to her. Did you see me do anything to her? For one thing, I'm practically sitting across the room."

The four of them lapsed into silence. Blaze stared out the window; Terry stared at Heather; and Heather started examining her hair, looking for split ends. Ashley wasn't staring at anything unless it was another world of her own creation. Everybody knew Ashley DeWitt was weird because of her mother. Ashley's mother was an artist who constructed sculptures out of car parts and dress mannequins. Mrs. DeWitt was famous.

When Gloria Crowley walked into the room, Heather looked sideways at Blaze. Terry, who had finally found his button in an oversized vest pocket, was trying to reattach it to his suspenders. Ashley sat up and propped her chin on her fists, looking at Ms. Crowley from under half-closed eyelids.

Ms. Crowley slammed her briefcase on the teacher's desk and stood in front of them, her arms crossed over her chest. She was wearing a scratchy-looking wool suit and a blouse buttoned up to her neck — uncomfortable, stiff-looking clothes. "Congratulations," she said, smiling down at the four of them. No one smiled back. "The four of you are the new members of this year's Yearbook Committee."

"There must be some mistake," Heather managed.

Gloria Crowley looked at Heather. "There's no mistake. You will be writing tag lines for every member of the graduating class."

"What's that supposed to mean?" Ashley mumbled.

"It means 'Most Likely to Succeed,' 'Cutest Couple,' 'Most Popular.' . . ."

" 'Most Likely to Be Followed and Tortured Horribly,' " Terry volunteered.

Ashley stared at Ms. Crowley. Ms. Crowley's face was stony. It had lines in it that weren't pretty. Anybody could tell just by looking at her that mercy wasn't a big item on Ms. Crowley's list of admirable personal attributes. Ashley sighed. She was getting a stomachache wondering what she'd done in a former life to be assigned to the Yearbook Committee.

"Hell!" Blaze slammed his hand into his desk with the practiced stroke of someone who knows how much violence to use in school — enough to be a statement, but not enough to send the desk sailing into the one in front of it. Blaze's eyes hardened, and he hitched his jacket onto his shoulders as he stood up and walked through the classroom toward the door. Terry, Ashley, and Heather watched in a detached way.

"Just where do you think you're going?" Ms. Crowley demanded.

"Hey, I have to be someplace, okay?"

"That's absolutely true. You have to be right here. Right now. For once you are in exactly the right place at the right time. Now, get back over there, and sit down." Gloria Crowley was glaring at Blaze.

Blaze picked a front desk in the row by the windows and dropped into the desk chair, feet splayed out into the aisle, a mocking grin flickering across his face. Heather looked at him and scowled. In Heather's opinion, Blaze Conrad was a cretinous mass. Terry was more Heather's type, but Heather wasn't looking to add any more male personages to her life: Last week she'd decided to thin out the ranks of her entourage. Being popular was just as much of a responsibility as being beautiful.

Meanwhile, Ms. Crowley was pacing back and forth in front of the classroom. "You may as well know, I've been through your files."

"I'm sure," Heather protested, betrayed.

"It's my job, Heather. Now, not one of you is a stupid person. You are all exceptionally talented and you all have a great deal of potential."

Blaze's face had turned hard and cold.

"There are lots of kids in this school with less natural talent than the four of you, but one thing makes them different. They get out there and use what they've got. Not a single one of you has participated in an extracurricular activity since you started at this school. That's inexcusable. You all know that you have to have at least *one* extracurricular activity to graduate. Maybe you were arrogant enough to think that we'd change the rules for you?" Ms. Crowley raised her eyebrows at the absurdity of the idea. "Rules don't change. Have any of you thought that you just might not graduate?"

No one had thought that.

"Or maybe you thought you'd slide through; that we wouldn't notice. Well, we did. We mean what we say. Any questions?"

Heather was wondering why Ms. Crowley's hair looked so weird. It was all stiff and glazed. If Heather had hair like that, she'd never walk out of the door in the morning. Other than that, there weren't any questions.

"I find it very surprising that none of you has anything you would like to ask," Ms. Crowley said nastily.

"We really have to do this, huh?" Terry confirmed.

"That's right." Ms. Crowley's mouth was set in a thin little line. She looked like she was enjoying herself. "The four of you are the most unmotivated, most uncooperative individuals I've seen in a long time. Every one of you has some kind of attitude problem, and I'm telling you right now that if you don't shape up, you're going to be in big trouble when you get yourselves out into the real world."

"Really?" Ashley asked, genuinely curious. Somehow she didn't see how Ms. Crowley's real world and her real world could ever exist simultaneously.

"Shut up!" Heather hissed. "If you ask questions like that, we'll be here all night."

"What's your problem, Heather?" Ms. Crowley demanded.

"The Yearbook Committee's beat," Heather complained. "Only jerks are on the Yearbook Committee. I mean, people practically have to be tied to warheads to do it."

"I'm sorry you feel that way, Heather, but whether or not you want to do this isn't the issue. You have no choice. I suggest that if you aren't happy with this situation, you just buckle down and get it over with. Now, on the bright side — "

"Just the side I was waiting for," Blaze interrupted.

". . . it'll be a little different this year. You're going to have some things no other Yearbook Committee's ever had."

"Phosphorous grenades?" Blaze suggested.

"You are all going to get last-period passes. Ten minutes off of every one of your last-period classes until the end of the year."

"Big deal," Terry shrugged. "I got study hall."

"As of this year there is an official Yearbook Committee room. You can do whatever you want with it as long as you don't deface or destroy the walls, floor, or ceiling." Ms. Crowley was talking like someone who is convinced that that was the first thing the four of them were determined to do, given the opportunity.

"Where's it at?" Blaze asked.

"It's the little room downstairs between the girls' gym and the furnace room. Room 228."

"It smells like dead socks and stale smoke in there," Heather sniffed.

"That's where everybody goes to sneak cigarettes," Ashley blurted.

The other three looked scornfully at her, and Ms. Crowley cleared her throat. "I am going to be checking on you. . . ."

"No joke. . . ."

"Because, Terry, I have a special interest in Yearbook."

Terry stared at Ms. Crowley in horror.

"All of you will be in the Yearbook room tomorrow at three-thirty. There will be no excuses for lateness or absence. Sickness is not an excuse," Ms. Crowley emphasized. "Do you understand me?"

They sat there miserably.

"Good." Ms. Crowley picked up her bag and walked out of the room.

As soon as she was gone, Terry stood up and began collecting his books. "No way she can make us do this if we don't want to."

Blaze wandered over to the door and started to drum on the chicken-wired glass pane. "You wanna bet?" He drummed himself out the door. "See you tomorrow."

Ashley

2

The next day after school Ashley was the first one to show up at Room 228. Even Ashley, who never paid a great deal of attention to where she was physically at any given time, thought the downstairs hall was depressing. It smelled like fifty years of boiled hot dogs. Halfway to the ceiling the walls were tiled with rust-colored squares and from the top of the tiles to the ceiling, the whole place was painted a strange creamy yellow. The last time Ashley had seen a color like that was when she'd turned over a frog to look at its stomach.

Ashley sighed and crept slowly down the hall in her purple high tops. The day had been depressing. She had woken up depressed, after having had terrible dreams all night about the Yearbook Committee. Ashley DeWitt had almost gone completely through this high school as an invisible underachiever and then, suddenly, here she was, assigned to participate. She'd ruined a perfect record of uninvolvement. Life just wasn't fair.

Ashley promised herself that once she got to

be eighteen she'd leave home and have an adventurous single life, making up her own rules as she went along. She'd dive to the bottom of interesting oceans, travel to remote places, and jump out of airplanes, but alone.

Ashley knew she wasn't perfect. For instance, she knew she lived in her head too much of the time. But then, lots of adults lived in their heads, too. Ashley knew her mother certainly did. Ashley's mother was an acclaimed artist, but people in town thought she was just weird. Ashley knew that if people thought her mother was weird, they thought Ashley was weird, too.

But as soon as Ashley took one look at the door of Room 228, she forgot all about being depressed and weird. The door was covered completely in brown wrapping paper, and scrawled across it in black letters was written: PLANET OF THE CREEPOID MUTANTS.

She knew all the stories, but Ashley hadn't taken them seriously. Last year a gang of seniors had cornered Susan Sakowitz in the parking lot and teased her with live garter snakes when they found out she had unofficially voted Jody Westlake "Most Likely to Need Electrolysis." It hadn't been Susan's fault. Everybody knew her mind was burnt out trying to come up with tag lines, but they did it anyway. That was the trouble with Yearbook Committee: It was too sensitive a job for anybody to do and live. This year's Yearbook Committee was getting picked on before they even *did* anything.

Ashley put her hands in her pockets and stared at the door.

"What're you doing?"

Ashley hadn't even seen Blaze walking down the hall. She shrugged. Blaze looked at her, walked over to the door. and ripped the paper off around the doorknob. Then he flipped it to the right and kicked the door open. Ashley followed him into the room.

For a couple of minutes Ashley watched Blaze walk around the room. He was wearing his normal uniform: black T-shirt, black jeans, black motorcycle boots, black leather jacket. He bounced on his toes. Blaze made Room 228 look very tiny. He had more energy than he could possibly use up in one lifetime, and all that energy took up a lot of space.

Room 228 was your basic orange. It contained a long worktable with four chairs. None of the chairs matched one another, and one of them lay on its side in the middle of the floor. The typewriter at the end of the table looked like it had time-traveled from the Mesozoic Era. The bulletin board on the wall facing the door was empty except for a couple of bent pushpins. Pushed into a corner of the room was a broken-down desk with the backrest unhinged from the seat. As Ashley looked around the room, the furnace next door turned over and a slow, steady vibration began to reverberate through the floor.

"Dump city," Blaze grumbled as he walked over to a corner and explored the contents of a carton abandoned the year before. He pulled out a box of stale Ritz crackers with a recipe for mock apple pie on the back; then there was a McDonald's Happy Meal container, a generous handful of golf balls that said RANGE, and a dart board.

Ashley sat down at the table to watch. "You believe somebody was actually in here eating Happy Meals?" she asked conversationally, trying to be agreeable.

Blaze grunted as he kicked the McDonald's container into the hall. "Yeah, well, they were big last year, Happy Meals. You bought a whole bunch of them and tried to figure out how many you could eat without throwing up."

Ashley got up and walked over to the door. She began to draw a tiny creepoid mutant in the corner of the wrapping paper with a brown marker she pulled from her knapsack.

Blaze looked up. "You can't see him very well," he said helpfully. "It's brown on brown."

"Protective coloration," Ashley said. Blaze wasn't paying attention to her. He was hauling a dart board out of the box. He stood up and started to bang the wall with his fists.

"What are you doing?" Ashley was curious.

"Trying to find a place to hang this thing, what else?" Blaze hauled his Swiss Army knife out of his boot and hammered a pushpin into the wall in a carefully chosen spot. He hung the dart board from the edge of the pushpin.

"It's holding." Blaze straightened the dart board and crouched in front of the carton. At the bottom of the carton, he pulled out a package of exacto blades and a roll of picture wire. He tossed them onto the table.

"*Now* what are you doing?"

Blaze sat down and started to construct throwing stars, wiring the exacto blades together two by two with the wire. He was humming to himself. He didn't explain. When he made four throwing stars, he picked one up and fired it at the dart board.

"Cute arsenal."

"You one of those nonviolent types?"

"No. I just don't go around making lethal weapons in my spare time." Ashley glanced at the floor. She wished the rest of them would get here. If they didn't pretty soon, she wasn't sure what she'd say.

But Blaze didn't seem to care one way or the other.

Ashley walked over to the table and sat down gingerly across from Blaze. His dark hair was in his face; he didn't look up. She folded her hands on the table and looked at her fingers; long, thin fingers with bitten-down nails. There was nothing to do, so she picked at her cuticle.

"You're going to make your fingers bleed, you keep that up," Blazed warned without looking up.

"So? What's it to you?" Ashley wished she could just disappear. She hated strange personal situations, and lately it seemed like her whole life was one big strange personal situation. She sighed desperately and pulled a *Zippy the Pinhead* comic book out of her knapsack.

"I figured at least Ms. Crowley would be here, anyway," Blaze grumbled. "I mean, what does she think we have, all day? She probably doesn't care." His face was practically right up against Ashley's eyes. He was smiling at her. "If you could be anything right now, what would you be?"

Ashley frowned. She didn't understand what Blaze meant. "You mean, like what kind of person?"

"Anything."

"From the past or present?"

"It doesn't matter."

"I don't know." Ashley took a deep breath. She'd never admitted this to anybody. "I guess I'd be someone very conventional."

"You're kidding me, right?"

Ashley blushed. "Well, you asked. What would you be?"

"When?"

"Now."

"Outta here."

"Oh."

"See, that's where we're different. I don't expect to *be* anything. Way I figure it, we'll get nuked or something, so why make plans and get disappointed?"

"Oh," Ashley said again, feeling stupid.

But Blaze hadn't finished expressing his opinion. "One thing I know I don't want to be, that's just like my parents. I'm never having any kids. People shouldn't have kids unless they're good at having them. Like, my parents should have thought twice, but they had to go right out without thinking about it and breed this family."

"How many brothers and sisters do you have?"

"Two."

"That's not many." Ashley didn't know if she really wanted to find out about Blaze's life. Everybody in school knew that he had a tough background. The kind of family that didn't have much money. Blaze came to school every day wearing the exact same thing, and he had a weekend job at the gas station. He didn't have many friends, and he was always getting into trouble. His father probably hit him. He did have a great bike, though, a black Harley he rode everywhere.

"Why?" Blaze turned around and glared at her. "How many kids in your family?"

"There's just me," Ashley admitted painfully.

"Well, at least they stopped right there. What's your father like?"

"I live with my mother."

"So what's wrong with that? You think you can talk louder? I can barely hear you."

Ashley was spared talking louder. Heather and Terry walked in the door. Heather stopped dead and surveyed the two of them. "Wonderful," she said. "Look who's here. It's Cycle Man and Weird Ashley." Heather looked around the room as Terry walked over to the table and sat down, grinning. "Why do I get the feeling I deserve more?" Heather sighed.

Blaze scowled. "I don't know, why do you?"

Heather ignored him and took a closer inventory of the room. "You know what? There's not even *one* single mirror in here," she complained.

"Look into my eyes," Terry suggested.

"I'd rather die. We really need a mirror."

"I'll get you a mirror," Terry offered in a burst of generosity.

"No, thanks." Heather removed a green plastic brush from her purse and began brushing out her hair. The bristles of the brush looked like green plastic nails.

"Don't you know that we're in serious trouble?" Terry asked her, leaning across the table.

"You guys may be in trouble, but as far as I'm concerned, I'm sure it's just a mistake I'm here. I'm not a failure like the rest of you. I've got early acceptance."

"Where?" Ashley asked.

"College, idiot. Where do you think? Unlike the rest of you, I'm motivated."

Blaze snorted. "Heather, you may be beautiful, but I hear you're slightly lacking in the brains department."

Heather spun around. "You'll be working at the gas station for the rest of your life. What do you know about brains? And as for you," Heather turned on Ashley, "you think you're magic because your mother's work is all over New York. Well, everyone knows your mother is a lunatic. And you're just as wacky as she is, the two of you living in that big asylum of a house on the edge of town. It's like some gothic horror show."

"It's just a normal house," Ashley mumbled.

Did everyone in the whole school really think she was a crazy person like her mother? Why couldn't she have a normal mother like other people, somebody who wasn't always painting in her studio, somebody who made cookies and casseroles, and cared about what to do with leftovers?

Ashley picked at the sleeve of her purple T-shirt. It was her favorite T-shirt, and it was fraying at the cuff. She'd spilled rapidograph ink all over herself in Graphic Arts this morning, and there was a big ink stain shaped like Africa just above her wrist. Ashley couldn't remember the last time she'd been so miserable.

"Hello, everyone. Blaze, why don't you stop crouching in the corner and sit down at the table with everyone else?" Ms. Crowley had arrived. Today she was wearing a white silk shirt buttoned up under a gray wool suit. She sat down at the head of the table and arranged several black pens, an official-looking notebook, and a stack of old yearbooks in front of her. "I'm sorry I was delayed; I was held up by a teachers' meeting. Let's get down to business, shall we?"

Ms. Crowley was fussing with the yearbooks. She paused and looked around the room to make sure everyone was paying attention. "I want to make sure you have some idea of what your responsibilities are. Your job is basically very simple, and if you settle down to work, it should take no time at all. Every student gets a tag line. After that, it's up to you. You might want to list special interests or extracurricular activities. You can also go with favorite sayings or likes and dislikes. You must, however, come up with an alphabetized list of seniors and captions, as well as photos for the 'Most Likely to' . . . a two-page spread at the end of the senior class section." Ms. Crowley opened the 1985 Yearbook and indicated the two-page spread. "That's it. The tag lines will be read at the Yearbook Dance, which you four will organize."

Ashley looked around the table. Heather, Blaze, and Terry all had glazed eyes. Nobody wanted to have to do this stuff. Ashley swallowed.

"What's the matter, Ashley?" Ms. Crowley was staring right at her, and it was no good trying to pretend she didn't exist.

"I don't think it's very fair," Ashley managed.

"What's not fair?"

"To label people like that and to have them read at a dance. What I think is that people are a lot more than just labels." Ashley looked away from Ms. Crowley just in time to see Heather rolling her eyes at Terry. Terry was smiling.

"I'm afraid that isn't a matter for discussion," Ms. Crowley said patiently. "The yearbook has traditionally had tag lines for its senior class. It will *always* have tag lines for its senior class, and every year there will be a group of students who will have to think them up. This year it's the four of you."

"Excuse me," Blaze cut in, "but Heather

seems to think that there's been some mistake about her being here."

"There's no mistake." Ms. Crowley was firm. Meanwhile, if Heather's eyes had been lasers, Blaze would have been vaporized on the spot.

"Are there any questions?"

"Do we *have* to do this?" Heather asked in a charming little-girl voice.

Ms. Crowley was not impressed. "This is the *last* time I'm going to tell you. None of you has a choice. You had a choice for four years. During that time, any one of you could have chosen *any* extracurricular activity in the world. Anything. You all know the graduation requirements. You could have gotten this over with freshman year. Since you didn't, we have been forced to assign you to Yearbook Committee. You may as well learn right now that, in life, making no choice is a choice."

They looked bleakly at her. If that was true, life wasn't going to be much fun.

"I guess we understand one another. You will meet in this room every Saturday morning and three afternoons during the week, until your work is done. There will be a member of the staff to check on you periodically and take attendance."

They all looked like they were in shock. "You didn't tell us about that part," Heather complained.

"The sooner you finish, the sooner your Saturdays will be your own," Ms. Crowley said grimly.

"What am I supposed to do about work?"

Blaze burst out. "I have to work at the gas station on Saturdays."

"I'm afraid you'll have to make other arrangements."

"I *can't* make other arrangements. I'm talking job."

"I'm sorry, Blaze, but you now have a prior commitment. Of course, if you'd rather, we'll be happy to have you back next year."

Ashley watched as Heather began to smile nastily.

"We'll be expecting you on Saturday." Ms. Crowley got up and left as the four of them stayed, wishing four varieties of violent death to the yearbook adviser at Prescott High.

Heather was the first to speak. She fingered the shoulderpads of her Norma Kamali dress and stared pointedly at Blaze. "I always wanted to spend eighteen zillion Saturday mornings cooped up in an orange room with a psychotic cyclist weirdo."

Apparently Blaze had forgotten about being upset over his job. He looked at Heather and grinned demonically.

"I don't even *know* you guys," Heather wailed.

"Looks like that'll change," Blaze suggested.

"You're one of the sickest people I ever met, Blaze Conrad."

"Don't take out all your aggression on me." Blaze flung another throwing star at the dart board. "I'm sure you can find a better use for it."

"It's okay, Blaze," Ashley offered. "She didn't mean it."

"Since when did you become an authority on what I mean and what I don't mean?" Heather snapped.

"It's okay, Ashley." Blaze ignored Heather. "I don't particularly care what some bratty rich kid thinks."

Terry stood up, smoothed down his hair, hitched up his pants, and picked his knapsack off the floor. "Well, I gotta get going."

"What's the matter, you too sensitive to stick around and watch the blood flow?" Blaze needled him.

"Confrontation gives him hives," Heather suggested.

"Yes, you're right," Terry admitted. "As a matter of fact, it does. Anybody coming with me?"

"Why don't you go with him, Heather?" Blaze suggested. "Terry could probably teach you a thing or two."

"Oh?" Heather's eyes flashed. "You don't know anything about me."

"Don't be so sure. We don't live in a vacuum, you know. I hear things."

Heather stood up, picked her brush off the table, and shoved it into her bag. As Blaze and Ashley watched her walk out the door, Blaze started to laugh. He laughed even louder when Terry followed her.

"Know what I think?" Ashley asked coldly. "I think that was a horrible thing to do."

"You do, huh?" Blaze looked unconcerned. "You haven't seen anything yet."

"It wasn't fair to pick on Heather like that."

"Who's picking on her? She started it. She was doing it to herself. Didn't you *see* her doing it to herself? Now what are you going to do? Turn it into a big thing or something? I never met so many sensitive people in my whole life."

"I *am* sensitive," Ashley said.

"It's hard to know what you are under all those baggy clothes you're always wearing," Blaze continued.

Right then and there, Ashley decided she didn't care what Blaze thought about her. "Look who's talking. Someone whose entire color palette is unrelieved black." Ashley's eyes were hot, banked coals in the fire of her face.

"Well, that's just what we need to top it all. Ashley DeWitt getting artistic temperament the first day."

Ashley glared at Blaze and stomped out into the hall.

"Ashley?" She could hear Blaze calling after her. "Wait up a sec, huh?"

But Ashley was walking fast, and Blaze had to find his Swiss Army knife. He picked it up, shoved it down the side of his boot, and hit the table with his fist. "Bunch of sensitives!" He kicked the chair Ashley had been sitting in across the room. Then he flicked off the light and banged the desk in front for good measure on his way out the door.

Meanwhile Ashley swept down the hall in a

rage, her boots pounding across the black-and-white linoleum floor. By the time she'd gotten to Prescott's west wing, she'd cooled down a bit. It seemed to take an eternity to climb the stairs and walk down the hall to her locker.

Mr. Chung, the Continental Geography teacher who spent most of his class time telling scary stories about his escape from Cambodia, was working late, doing whatever it was teachers did when they stayed after school.

"What's going on out there?" he asked as Ashley slammed her books onto the floor in front of her locker.

"Nothing."

"Is that you, Ashley?"

"Yes." Ashley dialed her locker combination and yanked the lock. The lock didn't budge.

"Are you all right?"

"I'm fine." Ashley leaned her forehead against the cool metal of her locker door and spun the tumblers again. She'd brought the lock all the way from junior high just so she wouldn't have to learn a new combination and, after five years, she still couldn't get her locker open on the first try. She was no good at anything. She might as well hang it all up; she was the biggest failure that ever lived.

Finally the tumblers clicked, and the lock opened. Ashley pulled open the door and dug around the bottom of her locker through old tests, broken pencils, gym socks, scarves, and fingerless gloves, until she hauled out her French book, which she managed to drag out by the cover and heave over her shoulder into her knapsack. She couldn't find her World History book. World History homework was due tomorrow, but Ashley figured World History had already waited about a couple of hundred years. A day or two more wasn't going to make a whole lot of difference.

Ashley slammed her locker shut, and Mr. Chung yelled, "Leave the walls for tomorrow."

Personally Ashley thought Mr. Chung had a rotten sense of humor. She walked down the empty hallway to the bus stop just in time to see the taillights of the last school bus heading off into the night.

Ashley decided then and there that she hated people. She wanted to live in a cave for the rest of her life. Terry was always flirting, Blaze was always mad at the world, Heather was unmentionable, and Ashley hated the whole idea of Yearbook Committee. First she'd had to sit there and listen to Heather being immature, not to mention Ms. Crowley, who'd probably gone into teaching because she enjoyed torturing people younger and weaker than herself. Then it had taken her several human lifetimes to get the locker open, feral beast that it was. Now here she was, the last living student at Prescott High School. She was totally stranded, watching the last school bus tooling down Lancaster Road.

Ashley pulled her knapsack onto her shoulders and began to trudge into town. She'd have to stand at the public bus stop and wait. Hardened criminals with rubber hoses would probably come and hit her and steal her bus pass. When they were done, they'd leave her in the middle of the road so horrible slimy night things could crawl out of holes to investigate her remains.

But before she knew it, Ashley was at the bus stop. She cheered up. There were three other kids waiting there: two girls and one boy. The girls were Ashley's age, and the boy was about twelve. They'd all missed the school bus, too. Ashley looked around for the criminals, but there didn't seem to be any lurking in the bushes. She was secretly disappointed; nothing in life ever turned out as she anticipated.

The two girls stood by the newspaper machine, smoking cigarettes and talking about boys and cars. The boy was hunting in his lunchbox to see if he'd really eaten his entire lunch already. He had.

"How long do you think it'll take the bus to get here tonight?" the blonde girl asked her red-haired friend.

"Don't know. You know?" she asked the boy.

"Couple of hours," he said matter-of-factly.

"What are you asking him for? He's only a kid. They have no sense of time."

"I do, too!" the boy said.

"I wish it would hurry up and get here. I want to get home," the red-haired girl whined.

"What's that noise?" the boy asked suddenly.

Everyone at the bus stop, including Ashley, turned around as a motorcycle came flying out of the night and stopped in front of them.

"Hi, Ashley," Blaze said.

Ashley looked at him.

"You missed the bus, huh? Do you need a ride home?"

"If she doesn't, I sure do," the redhead volunteered.

"You don't even know where I live." Ashley stepped away.

"Give the guy a break. Here he is like some vision on a Harley, and you can't get real?" The blonde girl despaired, questioning Ashley's sanity.

"Hop on, let's go." Blaze revved the engine.

The boy looked at Blaze for a couple of minutes. Then he looked at Ashley. "You know, what I think is you should take the ride. The bus takes hours. I'm not kidding. Anyway, it's starting to rain."

After a moment's hesitation, Ashley climbed onto the back of Blaze's motorcycle.

The two girls watched appreciatively as Blaze and Ashley rode off.

Blaze skidded to a stop at the next light. "You want to give me directions?"

What Ashley really wanted to do was figure out where to put her hands. She was too embarrassed to grab Blaze, but if she didn't, she'd probably fall off. Especially the way Blaze drove.

"Well?"

"You have to take a right down Frasier Crest."

"This rain's really starting to come down, huh?"

"Oh, yeah." Ashley looked up at the sky. "I

like rain," she insisted. The foggy drizzle had turned into a serious downpour, and Ashley's sweater was getting soaked. She smelled like a wet sheep dog.

At least Blaze solved the problem of where to put her hands. "Grab on to me and tuck your head into my back. That is, if you, uh, want to," he finished lamely. "How far down Frasier?"

"Pretty far."

"You guys really live out there, don't you?"

"It's my mother. She likes to be by herself so she can work."

When the light changed, they shot down the road, the cycle's engine roaring. Before long, the mudguards were clogged, and they breached mammoth puddles that dotted the newly grated two-lane road. Blaze turned on his headlight, and they cruised through the sloppy night, riding close to the median, dodging bumps and mud puddles.

Finally they pulled up to Ashley's house, an old, rambling farmhouse huddled against a stone wall that shadowed the road for the length of the property. The house was gray with red trim. Ashley and her mother had painted it that color last spring because Ashley's mother had never seen a gray house except for the weathered ones that started out being another color.

Ashley got off the bike. Her skirt flapped around her calves and stuck to her thighs like papier-mâché. "You can come in if you want," Ashley offered. "I mean, since you're wet and it's raining."

"I think I'll go on home," Blaze said.

They looked at each other, rain streaming down their faces. "Maybe I can stop by next Saturday. Give you a ride home or something," Blaze volunteered.

"Sure," Ashley said, going through the motions. She knew it would never happen. "Hope your bike's okay."

"I'll wipe it down when I get home."

"Well, good."

"Yeah. Best thing for a wet bike. You can't be too careful. You have to watch out for rust."

"Rust is nasty stuff," Ashley agreed.

"I gotta get home." Blaze kicked his bike back into life and spun around on the wet gravel. Ashley stood by herself, watching him bounce down the driveway and onto the road. She was wet and muddy, but it was better than waiting at the bus stop.

3

Ashley headed for the house, walked in the kitchen, and closed the door against the rain. For a split second, she leaned against the door and thought about Blaze. That was before she noticed the kitchen was incredibly smoky. It was her mother's ceramics kiln again. The warning light was flashing crazily, and smoke came streaming out the door. Ashley groaned and pulled the plug.

Ashley'd be really glad when "Love in the Ruins" was finished. "Love in the Ruins" was what Ashley called her mother's newest piece of work. Her mother called it something else, like "Mythic Directions." Mythic or not, it seemed like lately Ashley's mother hadn't been paying a whole lot of attention to her work. The sad part was that even when her mother didn't concentrate she was better at what she did than most people. A long time ago Ashley realized that her mother's work never really suffered, it was just accident-prone.

"I know, Ashley, I can smell it," Mrs. DeWitt hollered from her studio.

"I unplugged it already."

"Good girl. Get some pumpkin pickles and a can of vegetable soup from the cellar if you're hungry. I'm kind of tied up in here. I'll get something later."

Ashley wished that just once she could walk in the house after school and smell something that resembled a roast beef dinner. Some normal kitchen smell. Something other than burning kilns and chemicals.

She walked through the living room. It was a mess as usual. Her mother wasn't really dirty, she just collected piles of things for the visual pleasure it gave her. Ashley's mother was always threatening to redo the house completely one day. When she had the time. Ashley wasn't holding her breath, though. The idea was to see beautiful things wherever you looked, her mother said. Now Ashley mainly saw clutter. The shapes sort of went together, but if you looked closely, there was the moment of truth that told you all the objects in sight were less composed than a big salad.

For instance, over by the windows an antique Victorian child's dress hung on the wall next to a couple of photographs of long-dead Victorian DeWitts. The relatives were vacationing on a cruise ship. They all sat very stiffly around a table drinking tea and eating biscuits. Wise-faced parrots perched on their shoulders, and a tiny monkey huddled by Ashley's great-aunt's chair. Right next to the Victorian relatives was a watercolor of a Scotsman in kilts, a gigantic trout tied to his back. This was supposed to depict another relative, fishing in a romantic trout stream in the mid–1800s. Underneath the wall grouping was a cherrywood sideboard covered with seashells from the West Indies. All these things were supposed to go together conceptually, but they really made Ashley glad she didn't have any friends to invite over.

Ashley walked down the hall decorated with African masks, past the bathroom choked with shadowboxes of atrophied butterflies, to her own room. She went in and shut the door. Her room was perfectly bare. There were no curtains on the windows, the floor had been sanded down to a polished oak finish, and the walls were stark white. A white desk and chair were shoved up against the wall by the bed. Two futons, one on top of the other, were on the floor covered with a Hudson Bay blanket. The only real colors in the whole room were the black, red, yellow, and green stripes on the blanket.

Ashley felt safe in her room. Being there made her feel as if her life was manageable. The room was so bare, her mother never came in, maintaining that Ashley's room made her color-hungry.

Ashley stuck a tape in her tape deck on a shelf across from her bed. She was proud of that shelf. She'd put it up herself. She stripped off her wet clothes and pulled on a gray T-shirt, a pair of faded 501 jeans, and a gold-and-gray brocade vest that used to belong to her father, who had taken off long ago. Dressed, Ashley lay down on her bed and stared at the ceiling.

It wasn't that she really cared what people thought. Not really. Being Rhodi DeWitt's daughter made her instantly abnormal. The real problem was that her mother was such a tough act to follow. She'd have to grow up and be as great as her mother. People would expect it.

Ashley didn't know if she wanted a life like her mother's. Her mother worked all the time. Ashley was convinced living like that made a person unbalanced, and balance was very important to Ashley.

Ashley hadn't drawn one single thing in the last two years because she decided if she wasn't going to be good at what she did, she didn't want to do it at all. She decided that what she mainly wanted to do in life was become as invisible as possible. She'd been doing fine until Yearbook Committee. Now it looked like even that was no longer possible.

She sighed and rolled off the bed. She stuck a Drongos tape in her tape deck and sat down at her desk in front of the last yearbook, looking at the juniors. She'd made sure she was sick the day yearbook pictures were taken the year before. She'd also made sure she was sick all the days the make-up pictures were scheduled. Her picture wasn't in the yearbook at all: Her name was listed at the end of the junior class under Pictures Missing, with Stephen Pace, a guy who was seriously nowhere and wanted to become a Mountie; and Kenny Sandrussian, who'd had hepatitis all year.

Ashley was getting morose when, all of a sudden, she had an idea. She pulled out her red notebook and her twist-o-flex pen with the tiny stars on the side and started writing in alphabetical order: John Abisimira, "Best Arms"; Patricia Adamski, "Nicest Skin"; Marcia Aines, "Best Eyesight"; Sharon Alomoto, "Most Attractive Ankles"; Lou Anquist, "Blondest Hair."

Before long, Ashley had filled up two notebook pages, and it was eleven o'clock. Sure the tag lines were based on visuals, but how could she base them on anything else? She didn't know any of these people personally. About the only people she knew in a vaguely personal way were the four people who had been picked for Yearbook Committee. Two meetings hardly made it personal. Ashley didn't believe it was fair to judge people when you didn't know them. If you went around doing that kind of thing, other people would do it right back at you; that's how the world worked. People who got this yearbook were going to have it their whole lives. That meant their kids would see it someday. Who wanted to accept the responsibility for that? Who was she to give out these stupid tag lines? How could she take the consequences of calling somebody a nerd and run the risk of scratching a potential cultural hero? Just the thought of it made Ashley's palms sweaty and her head ache.

She read over the list. All right, so it mostly listed body parts, so what. And so what if there weren't enough parts of the human body to go around for a whole senior class. Maybe, once she took in her list, they could all add something. At least it was a start for the rest of the Yearbook Committee. And they wouldn't be listing things like "Most Likely to Fail Miserably and Not Even Notice," or "Most Likely Never to Cultivate One Single Redeeming Human Characteristic." That's the kind of stuff Heather would come up with.

Heather was an interesting person to watch from a distance, but Ashley didn't really know if she liked Heather or not. She supposed she didn't. The last thing Ashley wanted to do was to get to know Heather well enough to find out. Getting to know Heather was not what Ashley considered a profitable character-building experience. She'd rather eat car parts.

It was late, and Ashley was tired, and her head felt like it was spinning. She turned out the light, took off her jeans, and crawled underneath the Hudson Bay blanket in her socks and T-shirt with the radio on. It wouldn't be that long until Saturday. Of course, Blaze wouldn't come over on Saturday as he'd been saying, but at least he'd said it. She'd been there. She'd heard.

4

Saturday morning Blaze rode his motorcycle to school. Terry picked up Heather and gave her a ride. Ashley took the town bus. They were all sitting around the table in Room 228 when Ms. Crowley walked in to take attendance.

Ms. Crowley was looking casual in a pair of jeans with a crease ironed down the front and a completely unbendable white shirt that looked like it had been rinsed in leftover ruffle starch from the Elizabethan age. Ms. Crowley took the attendance and left. She wasn't feeling conversational.

Once she was gone, they sat around the table staring at one another. No one had much to say. Terry was fidgeting around in his chair as if he was being prodded with a hot wire. Heather was sitting next to him, touching up her mascara and eyeliner. Terry was trying to talk to her.

Blaze surveyed them all with a disgusted look on his face while Ashley tried to pretend she was an invisible speck on the floor underneath the worktable.

"So. Guys," Heather began, looking around the table without actually seeing any of them, "anybody do any official work?"

Ashley looked down at her feet. Last thing this morning she'd jammed her red notebook in her knapsack, but she wasn't going to admit it.

Blaze leaned back in his chair. "I decided Billy Vee is 'Weirdest of All Living Beings.'"

"Big deal. Everybody knows that. And he's practically at the very end of the alphabet," Heather announced as she dug around her bag for a magazine. She pulled out a copy of *Elle*, spread it out on the table in front of her, and leaned close to the page.

"You really take this stuff seriously," Terry said, leaning into her shoulder.

Heather jumped away, turned, and gave Terry a disgusted look.

"What's being at the end of the alphabet have to do with it?" Blaze demanded.

"I assume we're working in alphabetical order." Heather ran her fingers back and forth across a glossy page of yellow eye makeup.

Blaze shrugged. "So I'm working ahead."

Terry was hunched over, digging around the pockets of his jeans. "I got something here if I can just get it out," he grunted.

"People who insist on wearing skintight jeans should never keep important things in their back pockets." Heather flipped disinterestedly to the Spring Focus page.

"There!" Terry pulled out a sheet of paper and threw it on the table.

"Did you write all that?" Ashley asked. For a moment, she felt like she wasn't so weird after all.

"You kidding me? No way. Jennifer Delmotta did it."

"What is it?" Heather held out the scrunched-up, glue-puckered page disdainfully between her perfectly manicured fingers. "It's not even accurate."

"What are you talking about?" Terry demanded.

"Susan Ashford is *not* 'Most Glamorous.' Have you seen what she's been wearing this year? All those really faded clothes and everything? And she just let her hair go; I mean, she might as well have shaved her head. She used to have that British schoolboy look going for her, but she just lost it in spades."

"At least *somebody* did *something*," Terry protested.

"Right. You mean, Jennifer Delmotta did something, don't you?" Heather corrected.

"So. What's wrong with that?" Terry shot back.

"She probably did it for love, too," Ashley mumbled.

Heather looked at Ashley and snickered.

"Shut up, Heather. You think you're the last word on everything, don't you?" Terry said.

Ashley pulled her notebook out of her pack and ripped out her two pages. "Here."

Heather looked wordlessly at Ashley's face as Terry picked up the list and began to read out loud.

Ashley interrupted him. "It's just my rough thoughts. It really isn't anything. I tried to do something in case — "

"Do you believe it? She's actually apologizing," Heather observed.

Terry didn't stop reading. "John Abisimira, 'Best Arms'; Patricia Adamski, 'Nicest Skin'; Marcia Aines, 'Best Eyesight'. . . ."

" 'Best Eyesight'?" Heather protested.

"But she can read road signs from five blocks away; it's really true," Ashley said earnestly.

"You got that close to Marcia Aines to find out she has the best eyesight? She washes her hair with laundry detergent," Heather persisted.

"No, she doesn't," Ashley said stubbornly, her eyes fixed on the table in front of her.

"I like it," Blaze said. "But it seems to me that the trouble is you're concentrating on parts of the body here. I mean, you have some other stuff, but parts of the body is what you're telling us about. Thing is, you might run out of body parts. What's after arms and legs? 'Best Liver'? 'Best Sinuses'? 'Most Incredible Colon'?"

Ashley looked for a black hole in the floor through which she could disappear. "I know. That's exactly what's wrong, but I don't know how to fix it. I didn't want to be offensive. What do we know about these people?" Ashley looked around at them in confusion. "Haven't you ever gone through your parent's old year-books and read what other people said about them?" she asked desperately.

Everybody knew what she was getting at, but nobody would say anything. Terry looked uncomfortably at Heather, who was concentrating on her magazine. Blaze wouldn't look at anybody.

"All right, Ashley," Heather shot out. "Just stop it, will you? I feel guilty enough about my life without you tap-dancing on my conscience."

Blaze cleared his throat. "You're taking this way too seriously. We're only doing this because none of us has an extracurricular activity. We're not passing judgment on the world."

"But," Ashley argued, "it has long-term effects on other people's lives."

Blaze rolled his eyes. "Sure, Ashley."

Terry was looking at Heather in surprise. "What do you feel guilty about, anyway?"

"I don't feel like I'm a very good person. Is that all right with you?"

"Why?"

"I think that everything is always my fault, okay?"

"But I don't understand what you have to feel guilty about. For one thing, you're beautiful. You're maybe the most beautiful girl in the whole school."

"I'm not. I'm ugly. People expect beautiful people to be good, so I guess I'm ugly."

"How can you say that?" Terry was amazed.

"I don't know why I'm bothering to tell you

all this. I know it isn't my fault; I'm a really horrible person and practically the whole world's my fault." Heather looked like she was going to start crying.

"Are we allowed to leave the room around here?" Terry asked as Heather ran out into the hall.

There was nothing to do but wait for Heather to come back. Finally, when she didn't, Ashley got up and left to look for her. She found Heather sitting in the stairwell, blowing her nose into a white cotton handkerchief with lace trim. Ashley was amazed. She didn't think anybody in the world blew their nose on a handkerchief anymore. Heather's eyes were tearing up, and she was breathing funny.

"Are you okay?"

" 'Course not. Does it look like I'm okay? Just don't say anything to me, or I'll really start crying, and then my eyes will get all red and swollen, and I'll have to put cucumbers and ice on them for hours. Not to mention the fact that it took me practically twenty minutes to get the navy mascara on my bottom lashes this morning, and it's running already."

"Oh." Ashley stared at Heather. "But why are you breathing funny?"

"Breathing like this keeps you from crying."

"Really?"

"Yeah, you should try it. It works."

"But I thought crying was supposed to be good for you," Ashley said doubtfully. "You should let yourself cry."

"Why don't you just quit staring at me?" Heather suggested. "Better yet, why don't you just leave?"

"Okay." Ashley shrugged.

When Ashley got back to Room 228, Blaze looked up. "Well?"

"She's decided to be by herself," Ashley explained.

"Why?"

"How would *I* know?" Ashley was getting irritated.

"Don't you think she better get back in here before somebody official shows up?" Terry wondered.

"Hey, you want her back in here, you go get her," Ashley flared. "I'm not going to run back and forth all day long."

"Whoah!" Blaze put his feet on the worktable and leaned back in his chair. "The girl is getting nasty."

"Shut up, Blaze." Ashley curled up in her chair, crossed her legs, and folded her arms across her chest. She felt cold and miserable. It was only a matter of time until she turned into one of those people in B-movie sci-fi scenarios.

"You know" — Terry was trying to be laid back and conversational — "what I can't understand is why the Yearbook Committee is always being treated like it's this leper colony."

Blaze picked up a pencil and began to drum on the table.

"The Yearbook Committee is always these nerds, misfits, loners. People who are untouchable social outcasts and stuff like that," Terry went on.

"You happen to be on the Yearbook Committee," Ashley stated flatly.

"That's what I'm getting at. You know, everybody in high school thinks they're a misfit and don't belong."

"Oh, come on," Blaze said impatiently.

"Lots of people fit in," Ashley argued. "You know, like cheerleaders and jocks and the Homecoming Queen and, like, the Drama Club. . . ."

"The Drama Club?" Blaze stopped drumming long enough to explode into laughter.

"Shut up, Blaze," Ashley said.

"But, the Drama Club?" Blaze was laughing so hard, tears were practically pouring out of his eyes.

"See," Terry decided. "This is exactly my point."

"*What's* your point?" Blaze asked.

"Everybody in high school is convinced everyone hates them and spends all their time laughing at them behind their backs. See," he explained, "they all think they aren't as cool as other people, and everyone has a lousy self-image."

Just then Heather came walking in. She sat down beside Terry, looking droopy.

Nobody said anything. They sat in silence for a long time until Heather, out of nowhere, said, "You have to worry about being perfect."

"What's that?" Terry turned to look at her.

"It's not easy, having to be perfect. No matter what you do, you're never good enough."

Ashley looked Heather in the eye. "Try having a famous artist for a mother." She rubbed the top of the table with her index finger.

"You rub any harder," Blaze said, "you're going to break your finger right off at the knuckle."

Ashley put her hands in her lap and pulled the bottom of her sweater over them.

"Well," Heather looked breezily at her watch. "I'm really late for my facial. Maybe I'll see you guys around. Guess we can wrap it up for this morning."

Blaze looked at Heather speculatively for a couple of seconds. "Kinda shallow, aren't you, Heather?"

Heather was packing up her things. "I don't have anything more to say."

"I don't recall you saying anything particularly helpful all morning. Who knows what you were saying out in the hall, though." Blaze made a big deal out of giving Heather the benefit of the doubt. "You could have been out there just burning up the hall with all of these positive, wonderful thoughts."

"Yeah." Heather pulled her bag over her shoulder and walked out the door without saying good-bye.

"Now, there's a girl with a real commitment to her facial," Blaze said.

"Leave her alone, Blaze," said Terry.

"Hey, what'd I do? I didn't do anything, did I?"

"You'd better just leave her alone." And then Terry was out the door.

Blaze didn't look like he was in any hurry to leave, but Ashley knew she couldn't sit there any longer. How was she ever going to get through it, all closed up in here with the rest of them at one another's throats, afternoons and every Saturday morning until the end of high school?

"Alone at last, Ashley." Blaze's pen-drumming intensified.

"Don't make fun of me, Blaze Conrad." Ashley snapped.

"Who's making fun of you? I was about ready to ask you if you wanted to ride home."

Ashley didn't know what to say. He'd been serious about this all along.

"I thought maybe we could do something. That's if there's anything to do at your house," Blaze said.

It was her worst fears confirmed. A person she knew at school in her house. What was she supposed to say?

"Actually, I can talk to myself anytime; I don't know why I'm bothering to do it here," Blaze griped.

Ashley still had no response.

"Are you in there?" Blaze persisted. "It's Earth calling."

Ashley looked at Blaze and smiled weakly. "Yeah. I'm right here."

"That's a relief. Come on. Let's go."

"Okay." Maybe he didn't want to give her a ride home at all. Maybe he just wanted to see the inside of her house so he could make fun of her. What was she supposed to do about the fact that he was trying to haul her up out of her chair by the arm?

"*All right*," Ashley said, getting up herself. "Let's go."

There had to be some mistake. It couldn't be *her* walking down the hall with Blaze Conrad. Blaze walked halls alone. But he didn't seem to think it was weird at all. He was walking and talking just like it was any normal afternoon.

"What about your job?" Ashley asked.

"The job's okay. I work Friday night and Sunday now. I'm getting more hours than before. Before I just worked Saturday."

"What do you do there?"

"I overhaul Citroens."

"Really?"

"No. Really, I pump gas sometimes, and if there's a dynamite-looking woman in the car, I'll even do the windshield."

"Oh."

They were walking out of the school building. Ashley had run out of things to say already. "What gas station?"

"The one on the corner of Drucker. Why, you need your windshield cleaned?"

"I don't drive much. The car's always breaking down."

"What kind of car?"

"It's an old Pontiac. It's my mother's. People are always trying to get her to sell it, but she won't. She says she has this emotional attachment to it."

"The more cars break down, the more attached people get to them," Blaze said philosophically as they walked over to his bike in the parking lot.

He unlocked his bike, and Ashley watched the sun shining on his leather jacket. It was beautiful. It was so beautiful, she didn't notice he was waiting for her to climb on behind him.

"You coming now, or waiting for the five-fifteen?" Blaze asked sarcastically.

"Oh, yeah. Sorry."

"Keep your legs away from the exhaust pipe. You'll probably burn holes in your jeans if you don't. And I don't know how you think you're going to stay on this thing with your hands in your pockets like that; you're not even grabbing with your knees."

Ashley put her hands around his waist. "How long have you had this bike?"

"A couple of years. My father bought it, actually. Then, when he got his new touring bike, he gave it to me."

"Oh."

"My father's always owned a bike."

"Got you." Blaze's father was probably a biker turned trucker or something. He probably came home every two weeks and parked his rig in the driveway, and Blaze and his family ate Ring Dings and TV dinners while they watched football games with him. That made Ashley feel better. Blaze probably wouldn't think her house was too weird. Most likely he wouldn't think it was all that normal, but then, his house probably wasn't all that normal, either. As they started down Lafayette, Ashley began to relax.

It was a windy, raw, late spring day, which only made the ride more exciting. Ashley was lost. She was fantasizing about Blaze, on his bike, with the wind in his hair, taking her off to have adventures. Then they pulled up into her driveway. "That was a short ride," she said, despite herself.

"I found a shortcut on my way home the other day." Blaze eased the bike up next to the garage and whooped as he got off. "Who's that over there?"

Ashley looked in the direction he was pointing. She turned red.

It was her mother. She was out behind the garage blowtorching something to death. Rhodi DeWitt was wearing large gloves, a flameproof vest, goggles pulled down over her eyes, army pants, and huge black rubber boots.

"That's my mother."

"That?"

"Yeah."

"I can't believe it. That's incredible." Blaze was getting very excited.

"You get used to it," Ashley offered.

"Get used to it? I love it." Blaze was off, hopping through the weeds like a young dog about to catch its first Frisbee. Ashley followed him more slowly. When she caught up to Blaze and her mother, Mrs. DeWitt had shoved her goggles up off her face and was deeply involved in an explanation about how the blowtorch worked, patting the sleeve of Blaze's leather jacket now and then for emphasis.

"Everything go all right this morning, Ashley?" Mrs. DeWitt was smiling.

"Fine. It was fine. Blaze gave me a ride home."

Blaze was smiling, too. "Ashley offered to show me around."

"That's interesting. Ashley doesn't bring many friends home. She used to have a friend named Sarah who came over sometimes, but her father was transferred, and we haven't seen her in a long time. I'm afraid I'm not exactly up on all of Ashley's friends." Mrs. DeWitt was making it sound like Ashley's friends numbered in the rough vicinity of a cast of thousands.

"Well, I'm really glad she let me come over this afternoon, that's for sure," Blaze offered.

Ashley had never seen Blaze so enthusiastic about anything. "We've sort of become friends through Yearbook Committee," he was babbling on, "which was something none of us wanted anything to do with."

"Oh?" Mrs. DeWitt looked puzzled. "I thought it was a great thing for Ashley to be involved in."

"None of us wanted to do it," Blaze was explaining. "We were all forced. On account of none of us can graduate without an extracurricular activity."

"Ashley didn't tell me about that."

"It's no big deal," Blaze hurried on. "It's just a pain. Like, I had to change around my job hours and everything."

Ashley stood out in the yard behind the garage while Blaze talked to her mother. Ashley had néver expected this. Blaze actually *liked* her mother. If he didn't, he was sure putting on an amazing act. Ashley was hoping he wouldn't go anywhere near the inside of the house. Even if Blaze's father was a trucker, Ashely didn't want to spring the inside of the house on him right away.

Blaze stayed for the entire afternoon talking to Ashley and her mother. He stayed for supper. When Mrs. DeWitt suggested he call home, he shrugged and looked at his plate. "They don't care."

Ashley kicked her mother under the table. Of course Blaze's family didn't care if he came home for dinner or not. They probably had barely enough food to eat as it was. It probably meant his brothers and sister got extra. Meanwhile, Blaze wouldn't say another thing about his mother or any member of his family. He just took three helpings of stew.

It was a mystery to Ashley why her mother had taken it into her head to make stew this morning, but she had. Blaze would think they ate like normal people all the time. Ashley smiled gratefully at her mother who, of course, immediately misinterpreted the whole thing.

Mrs. DeWitt patted Blaze on the shoulder after dinner. "Stop by again, Blaze. Ashley's been so much happier today. Usually she doesn't say much at all."

Ashley refrained from pointing out that she'd hardly said anything; Blaze and her mother had done most of the talking.

They walked Blaze to the door. "Well . . ." Mrs. DeWitt said, as they watched him waving from the road, ". . . he's a curious kid. I wonder why he feels so uncomfortable about his family background."

"I don't know," Ashley shrugged. She didn't know what was happening at all. She felt as if she was losing total and complete touch with reality. Blaze had liked her place so much Ashley was sure he was practically getting ready to move in.

5

Although Ashley didn't expect much from Blaze, she walked around feeling like she had prisms stuck in her eyeballs. The world was really beautiful.

Blaze talked to her every single day. Well, not talked, exactly. Monday he grabbed her by the back of her jacket in a crowd of kids on the front steps. Tuesday, third period, he opened the door for her between the old and new wings and asked where she was heading. It wasn't as if he really wanted to know; he didn't stick around long enough to wait for the answer. Wednesday, he met her by the phones and squeezed her arm just above the elbow. Ashley turned around in time to see him running down the hall through a crowd of students, his leather jacket flying out behind him.

It seemed as if every time Ashley managed to become semifunctional, Blaze would show up again. She didn't know what was going on. She felt like she was turning into a new person. Her whole world seemed to be changing.

At least, it was changing until Friday after school. Friday after school it all came crashing down again. Mary Zambruski told her to wise up and watch where she was walking when Ashley crashed into her coming up the second stairwell. And then she'd almost put Leonard Tesser's eye out with her elbow when she'd tried to catch the kamikaze clipboard that shot out of her locker, embedding itself between the wall and the baseboard right under Kenny Durea's inflatable robot that was taped to the inside of the locker.

Ashley threw the clipboard back onto the top shelf of her locker. She pulled her fuchsia scarf off its hook, wrapped it around her neck three times, and pulled on her oversize man's tweed jacket. She jammed all of her books into the bottom of her locker and kicked the locker shut.

That's when she noticed the note taped to the front of her locker, just below the air vent. It was folded up real tiny. A wide strip of tape covered most of its surface. The note looked like a square spitball. When Ashley peeled it off, flakes of locker paint came with it.

Ashley unfolded the message. It was on a large sheet of notebook paper with a black border drawn around the page's edge. Some of the note was printed in black magic marker, and some of it was made of cutout letters from magazines. As she read it, Ashley felt like a dinosaur was dying a slow and painful death inside her stomach.

Freak:

You think Blaze Conrad likes you? He doesn't like anybody. But so what, you're both Mutated Garbage, anyway. The Point is this: Some people are very concerned about the yearbook, and some people are very worried you'll screw it up. Don't screw up. It would be bad for your health, mental and otherwise.

Ashley held the note close to her chest as she read it again. When she was finished, she folded it in half lengthwise and looked around the hall to make sure nobody had seen her. As far as she could tell, nobody had noticed. The hall was clearing fast. If she didn't get moving there would be nobody else left in the entire hall except for Leonard Tesser, who was always the last person to leave Prescott High. It was as if he practically waited for the sun to rise in Japan before he went home. Leonard spent most of the day glued to his locker. Maybe he knew who had stuck the note to her locker door.

Ashley walked over to Leonard. Leonard was crouched down on the floor in front of his locker. At least his legs were. Most of the rest of him was inside the locker. Ashley crumpled up the note and shoved it down into the bottom of her bag with the tropical fruit Life Savers, leaky pens, and eraser bits.

She leaned up against the locker next to Leonard's and stared down at his back. His shirt had come untucked from his jeans. Ashley could see a large expanse of the whitest skin in the whole world banded by the elastic tops of his jockey shorts.

"Leonard?"

A muffled sound that could have been a "What?" came out of the locker.

Ashley bent down at exactly the same time Leonard decided to stand up. The top of Leonard's head smashed into Ashley's chin. It hurt more than Ashley ever thought possible. She was glad she had a high threshold for pain.

"*Leonard*, watch where you're going, can't you?"

"Do you think I have eyes in the back of my head or something?" Leonard complained. He stood up, holding a large mason jar full of water in his hand. In the jar was a tiny, water-inflatable red robot that could grow to twenty times its size when immersed. Leonard looked at the jar critically and shook it experimentally. Bubble condensation from the robot's skin rose to the surface of the water in slow trails.

"Look, Leonard, I'm sorry to bother you and all," Ashley said, eyeing the robot, "but I have to ask you something kind of important."

"What?" Leonard said absently.

"Did you see anybody hanging around my locker this morning?"

"Nope." Leonard turned the jar over, and the robot took a dive, bouncing off the bottom on its fists.

"Come on, Leonard, this is important."

Leonard looked briefly at Ashley. "They inspecting lockers again or something?"

Ashley shook her head.

"So, what's the problem?"

"I just wondered if you saw anything strange going on over at my locker, is all."

"What's strange? You missing something?"

"You think I'd come around asking *you* if I were?"

"Could be you're missing this?" Apparently satisfied with the results, Leonard shoved the jar back into his locker. Then he reached up to the top shelf and pulled out an envelope with Ashley's name typed across the front. He handed it to Ashley and smiled. It was a horrible smile. It showed all of Leonard's braces.

Ashley stiffened.

"It was hanging out of your locker vent," Leonard explained. "I saved it for you."

"Thanks." Ashley grabbed the envelope out of his hand.

"So, be that way." Leonard shrugged.

Ashley folded up the envelope and put it in her pocket. Slowly she walked across the hall and pulled out her French workbook with the red smile-face on the front. The envelope felt like it was burning a hole through her pocket, but she didn't dare to pull it out until she was someplace private. She went into the girls' bathroom, maneuvered her way around the row of girls three-deep in front of the mirror putting on makeup, and locked herself in one of the stalls. The whole bathroom smelled like the Charlie counter in a department store. Ashley pulled the note out of her pocket and ripped it open. Inside was a piece of notebook paper. Typed across the page in capital letters was:

YOU AREN'T SO SMART. I'M ON TO YOU.

That was all. Ashley felt itchy all over her body. She felt like she was going to throw up. Mechanically she shoved the note into the bottom of her purse and swallowed hard against the lump in her throat.

Ashley didn't know anybody well enough to have an enemy who sent her notes.

Terry

6

Friday after school, while Ashley was finding hate notes in her locker, Terry was sitting in Dolores's room, watching her slip hooks into several earrings and hang them in her multiply pierced ears. Dolores was Terry's best friend. She was wearing a baggy black sweater and stirrup tights. Some kind of death-white lipstick with a pale pink sheen was painted on her mouth.

Terry was sitting on the floor, leaning up against Dolores's bed, a bag of potato chips in his lap and some sour cream and chive dip beside him. He was wearing a red T-shirt and a pair of Levi's 501 jeans. Dolores had given him the T-shirt for his birthday.

"I don't care what you say, Terry, you've never hated parties before. So why are you so down on the one we're going to tonight?"

Dolores turned her head, admiring herself in the mirror. "Which earring do you like better? I mean, really. Do you like the plastic banana or the pink crystal?"

"I don't know. I guess the pink crystal."

"Yeah, but is it really dynamite or just sort of fine? Come on, Terry, I depend on you."

"I like it. I said I like it, didn't I?" Terry rattled the potato chip bag.

"What's eating you, anyway? You're a real pleasure to be around lately, you know that? And all this week you've been stuck in that Room 228 after school. I mean, I really don't see what the big problem is. There's not that many seniors in the school, right?"

"Yeah."

"And all you have to do is come up with something to say about each one of them. You get a 'Most Beautiful,' a 'Most Successful,' 'Best Couple,' that kind of trash, and bingo, you're through. You guys are taking this whole thing way too seriously if you ask me. You should think of it as fifties retro, all get in this big room for a couple of days with some bebop music, write some things down, and you'll be done in no time."

"It's not that easy."

"So, what's so hard?" Dolores flounced over to her standing mirror and tried on a black velvet beret. "I hate it when you get like this. It's like palling around with Dracula." She pulled the beret low over her eyes and pursed her lips in the mirror. "So what do you think?"

"About what?"

"This hat. Does it add anything, or should I just forget it?"

"You gotta understand. It's not like just coming up with tag lines for each person. You gotta think about the fact that while you're on the

Yearbook Committee you're on everybody's primo hate list. No matter how hard you try, *somebody's* going to hate you for what you call them. And then we have to get everybody to agree on everything. Getting the four of us to agree is worse than trying to decide what twelve people want on one pizza. We're not exactly your natural group."

"Well, you're right about that." Dolores smiled and blew kisses to herself in the mirror.

"And then there's the dance."

"What dance?"

"You know, the Yearbook Dance they have every year to announce the tag lines. We're supposed to organize the whole thing."

"Nobody takes that seriously, Terry," Dolores said, trying to be consoling. "And anyway, Heather Mercer was born to organize social events. I mean, that's what she's spent her whole life training to do. Just make *her* do it. What's the story on Ashley? Is Ashley's mother really as weird as everyone says?"

Terry helped himself to more potato chips. "How am I supposed to know? I've never laid eyes on Ashley's mother. Why?"

"Everybody says she's really strange."

"Strange?"

"Yeah, well, look at Ashley. She's not exactly rooted to the ground."

"You're overdramatizing."

Dolores flicked black mascara onto her eyelashes. "Hey, I'm just a dramatic sort of girl, what can I say? Do you think I should get my eyelashes dyed? Heather Mercer gets her eye-lashes dyed."

"Does it hurt?" Sometimes Dolores got funny ideas. He watched as she bent more closely to the mirror to tone up the eyeshadow underneath her bottom lashes.

"Probably not, but it's dangerous. At least that's what somebody in the bathroom said. It can blind you if you get it done wrong."

Terry pulled tufts of carpet fuzz out of Do-lores's pink wall-to-wall carpet. "There's got to be a simple way to deal with this whole thing," he said, half to himself.

"Well, I wish you'd figure it out. Maybe then we can actually go out and *do* things again. We haven't had any real fun in a long time, Terry. You've been really preoccupied lately. And we don't hang out anymore like we used to."

"You know, Heather's so beautiful it's like she's not even human. It's scary."

Dolores nodded. "Yeah. I know what you mean. It's too bad she's so stupid. That girl could have the world at her feet if she just had one or two connecting brain strands. You keep looking at her, expecting to see smoke coming out her ears from the electrical fires caused by her brains shorting out."

Terry got an idea. "Girls always like me, right?"

"Yeah, so."

"I mean, Jennifer and Lisa and Christine like me a lot, don't you think?"

Dolores nodded.

"What if I just talk one of them into doing the whole thing? Would that be so bad?"

"What whole thing?"

"All the tag lines."

"*And* the dance, *and* the prizes? Everything?"

"No, we can do the dance and the prizes."

"Let me just get this straight." Dolores swiveled around toward Terry and put her hands on her hips. "Are you trying to tell me that some poor girl, out of pure love for you, is going to do the whole job that Crowley put four seniors on? I can't believe you, Terry. I mean, I've heard about ego, but this really beats it. It's like sometimes you act like this person I don't even know."

"But it would make the girl happy. I mean, I know that sounds really awful and everything, but it would." Terry gave up. "You just don't understand."

Dolores set her death-white mouth in a line and shook her head. "You wanna bet? Why do you think Abe Stillman is overhauling my Firebird?"

"You kidding me?"

"What's your problem?" Dolores asked defensively. "You're doing the exact same thing, only worse. Anyway, what I'm doing is a lot better than what you're doing."

"Why?"

"I happen to really like him."

Terry shrugged. "Who says I don't like Jennifer, Christine, or Lisa? I like them. They're really sweet girls."

"Stupid, too. Guys are cute when they're dumb and in love. Dumb girls in love are just being suicidal."

"I don't know," Terry shook his head. "I don't think it's such a bad idea."

"As an idea it's fine. As something you're going to do to another human being, it has its problems." Dolores got up and pulled Terry's hand. "Come on, I want to get on over to the party."

Dolores drove down Sanbourne Street like a maniac, checking her watch every two seconds. "We're really late. Of course," she tried to convince herself, "Jeremy's parties are always late. They start late."

Terry sat folded in on himself in the passenger seat and listened to Dolores. Terry liked girls a lot, but sometimes Dolores made him tired. She had a high energy level, and she was always talking.

Finally Dolores turned down Jeremey's street, and Terry stuck his head out of the window. "Check it out. What's going on?"

Dolores pulled up in front of the house. Roughly fifteen cars were parked up and down the street, and about thirty-five kids were standing in the driveway. No one was laughing. There was no music. Jeremy was standing in the middle of his driveway with a crowd of people grumbling around him. Terry could hear Jeremy, who never shouted, starting to yell.

Terry and Dolores got out of the car and walked past two girls standing on the lawn, talking. Terry overheard one of them say, "I always knew Jeremy didn't have it entirely together. His stuff never pans out."

"Yeah," her friend agreed.

"I mean, what kind of idiot throws a party the night his parents come home from vacation, anyway?"

The crowd was starting to break up in twos and threes.

People were wandering off to their cars. Dolores and Terry managed to corner Jeremy. "What happened?" Dolores demanded.

"My parents came home."

"In the middle of the party?"

"Actually, it was sort of toward the beginning."

Terry was looking around. There wasn't really anybody here he wanted to talk to, although people kept coming up to him with condolences for getting stuck on the Yearbook Committee. All of Terry's friends knew why he'd never gotten around to having an extracurricular activity. Who else could have six dates with six different girls on one night and not have any of them find out for three whole days?

Cindy Rinaldo sidled up to Terry and bumped his leg with her hip. "Hi, Terry."

Terry looked down at Cindy, who was small and darkly beautiful. Cindy's smoldering eyes were fascinating, even though Terry knew she could turn them on and off at will.

"I hear you're on the Yearbook Committee." Cindy smoothed her jeans with the flat of her palms.

"That's right."

"So tell me. Who am I?"

"I don't know, Cindy. Who are you?"

"I mean my tag line," Cindy said earnestly. "Did you decide on my tag line yet?"

"Not really." Terry sighed. "We aren't at the R's yet."

Cindy leaned more closely. "Why don't you make me 'Most Like Madonna'?"

"Why?"

"If you make me 'Most Like Madonna,' I'll get you guys free passes to my brother's club."

Dolores was suddenly eavesdropping. "The Underground?"

"Well, yeah."

"I hear the Underground is highly overrated."

Cindy shrugged. "Take it or leave it."

"I don't know, Cindy," Terry began. "You kind of look like Madonna in some lights, but I wouldn't say the resemblance is overwhelming. I don't know."

"It might be something you want to bring up sometime." Cindy winked. "You know what I'm saying? Maybe the others would feel differently," she finished, glaring at Dolores. "Whatever. See you around." Cindy was driving her father's Mercedes for the night. She got in, slammed the door, and floored it.

"Cindy's mad," Terry said to no one in particular. Yearbook Committee was going to destroy his carefully balanced social standing. He could see the signs.

"It's okay," Dolores said, trying to cheer him up. "She has a fat stomach, anyway."

Terry looked at her.

"Cindy Rinaldo," Dolores explained. "She has a fat stomach. Quite *unlike* Madonna."

"Yeah." Terry was unconvinced. He watched Dolores wander away and stand under a tree with Jeremy. It was okay that the party was off. Terry didn't really want to go to a party tonight, anyway. He was partied out.

"Yo! Wallace." Barreling across the lawn was Caldwell Prescott. Caldwell's father owned the town. Caldwell had been a frat boy from the day he was born. He had black hair and incredibly blue eyes. "How's it going?"

Terry stared at Caldwell who, up until now, had never said more than two conversational words to the likes of Terry Wallace.

But that didn't stop Caldwell, who was violently shaking his hand. "Heard about Yearbook Committee, chump." Caldwell threw an arm around Terry's shoulders and steered him toward the edge of the driveway, away from what little crowd was left. "Listen, I think I have a deal for you. Interested?"

Terry didn't have a chance to answer.

"It's a package deal. We're talking real money and a junior membership to Prescott Country Club for everyone on Yearbook Committee. All you have to do is name me 'Most Likely to Be Head of a Company Before Age Twenty-five.' Whaddya think? Is it doable?"

"I don't know, Caldwell." Terry was stalling.

Anger flashed across Caldwell's face. "So we give you a little time to think about it."

"You can give me as much time as you want,

but I don't know if it's going to make much difference."

Caldwell was nothing if not smooth. "So, hey, I'll see you around. Let me know."

"Yeah." Terry was unenthusiastic. Yearbook Committee was becoming a problem. What Terry didn't understand was why he was becoming Network Central. Did he look like a naive and gullible person? If so, he was going to have to do something about it, and fast.

"Terry! I can't believe it! You actually showed up." Terry didn't even have time to turn around before he found himself looking down into the face of Lisa Donnelly.

"Hi, Lisa." It was his chance. Terry was so happy he couldn't believe how lucky he was. "I was looking all over for you. What I was thinking was maybe you'd like to head over to that McDonald's on Duir Place. It's close. We could have some time to be alone and talk. Then we can come back here."

Terry had to come back there. He had no choice. Dolores had the car.

"Sure." Lisa looked like she was hearing music not normally audible to human ears.

"Okay if we walk over there?"

"Absolutely."

Terry started walking down Jeremy's street. At first, Lisa hesitated. She was making sure people saw her leaving the party with Terry. Then she caught up with him. Terry smiled down at her. "I have to tell you what it was like to see you getting off the bus last Friday."

"It was raining really hard last Friday."

"You were glowing."

"Growing?" Lisa sounded confused.

"G-L-O-W-I-N-G," Terry spelled. "You came walking into school all glowing with the rain dripping off your hair. You were clutching your books, and the ink on your notes was all running."

Lisa had a strange expression on her face.

"It meant something to me, seeing you like that," Terry finished lamely. "You know, I have something very important to talk to you about."

"Okay, but we'll come back to this growing stuff, right?"

"Yeah, sure."

They walked across the parking lot, which was jammed with cars. Terry pulled the door of McDonald's and held it open with his foot as Lisa walked in ahead of him. Terry realized he was starving. It was probably the stress of the situation, he decided, as he took Lisa's elbow and piloted her into a place in the shortest line. "Get anything you want, I got enough money here for whatever you want to eat."

"Actually, I think I'll just have a Diet Coke."

McDonald's was really noisy. Some five-year-old was having a birthday party, and it was hard to walk around without stepping on a kid or popping a balloon. They waited at the counter for their food and tried not to do a lot of moving around. Lisa wasn't exactly saying a lot. She was standing there with a nervous, dazed look on her face, staring at Terry when he wasn't watching.

"Come on," Terry said when they got their food, heading over to the only table in the dining room not inhabited by five-year-olds. "I need a little favor. It's no big deal, like I was trying to tell you before. And I can help you." He sat down and waited a couple of minutes, to be polite, before picking up his Big Mac and starting to chew through it. "See, what I really need is this person to help me out with this project."

Lisa sipped her Diet Coke. "Yes?" A paper airplane flew over her head and landed on the table.

"It might take some time, but it's interesting. Something you'd probably like." Terry noticed Lisa's hand inching across the table toward his. He brushed a piece of lettuce off the table and moved his hand away. "You sure you don't want a bite of this?" he asked, holding out his mangled hamburger.

"No. Thanks."

"What I need you to do is get hold of a copy of last year's yearbook. I mean, an extra one. Don't use yours, because you have to cut it up."

"Cut it up?"

"Yeah. What I had in mind was cutting out all the faces."

"What for?"

"Well, to put them in alphabetical order. After you think up something to say about each of them. Like, you know, 'Best Dressed,' 'Most

Sexy,' that kind of stuff. I know it'd be really easy for someone like you because you have this incredibly intuitive brain."

Lisa looked confused. She wasn't falling for the incredibly intuitive brain stuff. "Isn't that what the Yearbook Committee's supposed to do?"

"Well, yeah. But they do other things. Arrange for the Yearbook Dance. You're just helping with the prelims, see? And it's not like I'm asking you to do it all by yourself. I mean, I'll help. Who knows? This could be our chance to get to know each other better. I've been trying to think of a way to work it out so we *could* get to know each other better for a long time."

"What's wrong with asking me out?"

"I didn't want to do that. You know how it is, asking somebody out. It's a big thing. You don't get a chance to really get to know the person all that well. It's kind of an artificial situation. I want it to be natural with us. I like to think of you as a natural-type girl."

Lisa wouldn't look at him and, for a moment, Terry felt guilty. It didn't last.

"Okay, forget finding the yearbook. *I'll* find the yearbook. And I'll bring it over to your house or something, and then we'll sit around and you can help me. What do you think?"

Lisa played with her straw. "I don't know."

Sometimes girls could be really difficult. "I just thought it might be something you'd be interested in doing. I can always ask Nancy Weinberg or something."

"No. I'll do it. It's okay."

"You sure? I don't want to pressure you or anything."

"It's okay." Lisa sounded irritated. But it couldn't be helped. "I want to help you out."

"Good." Terry smiled and checked his watch. The next problem was going to be figuring out how to get home. Dolores had the car. Meanwhile, Lisa was neatly piling up all the garbage on a plastic tray.

"What else do you want to do before you take me home, Terry?" she asked him, clear-eyed.

"Actually, Dolores gave me a ride to Jeremy's. If we can get back there and find her, I'm sure she wouldn't mind giving you a ride, too."

Lisa sighed, squared her shoulders, and stood up. There was a funny look in her eyes. "All right." She looked like a person who had suddenly seen the truth and decided she could probably force herself to live with it.

7

The next morning when Terry woke up, he could hear his father yelling at his mother in the kitchen. Terry flinched. He reached over to the folding chair beside his bed and picked up the clock. The alarm hadn't gone off. He still had time to make it to the Saturday morning Yearbook Committee in time for attendance, but he'd have to move it.

Listening to his parents screaming at each other didn't make Terry want to get up. Usually on the weekend it didn't start until Sunday afternoon. It was going to be a long weekend. Not only that, Terry knew that if he was smart, he'd sleep over at Tom Sargent's tonight. With his father like this already, Terry knew it wasn't a good idea to be around the house later.

After really bad weekends, his father would buy them all presents. But the things Terry desperately wanted, like the VCR and the Panasonic video camera, seemed like pieces of junk metal when they showed up outside Terry's closed bedroom door late Monday night. It had been worse when he was smaller. Now that Terry had gotten to be almost his father's size, his father didn't bother him as much as he used to. But Terry remembered. When Terry was seven, his father had thrown him across the kitchen table vowing to teach him a lesson. All Terry had done was spill milk on the floor.

The kitchen door slammed, and the house filled with an unearthly quiet. Terry looked out the window and saw his mother backing the family Rambler out of the driveway. Sooner or later, Terry always figured his parents would get divorced. It used to worry him. It didn't anymore. Now he wished his parents would just get it over with.

What made his life even worse was that nobody at school knew anything about what went on at home. Sometimes it made Terry feel like he had two different lives. At school he had lots of friends. They liked him because he knew how to have a good time. But deep down inside Terry was afraid. The world didn't seem like a very comfortable place, and Terry suspected he wasn't tough enough. He wished he were a different kind of person. If he were tougher, none of this would be happening. He could do something about his father. As it was, he had trouble looking his mother in the eye because he felt guilty about the fact that he couldn't do anything to protect either one of them.

Ever since Yearbook Committee, Terry wished he could be like Blaze. All Blaze had to do was walk into a room and people left him alone. If things really got to him, Blaze just got on his cycle and tore around town. And if somebody gave him trouble, Blaze took care of it.

Terry pulled on his jeans and the army shirt he'd thrown over the set of weights and barbells in the corner of his room. No way he was sticking around long enough this morning to take a shower. If he was lucky, he could make it out of the house before he ran into his father. Right now his father was probably in his office going through a pile of paperwork. He did the same thing every weekend. Terry figured it was a desperate attempt to keep from tripping up on his fast-track job.

Terry pulled his boots out of the closet and left his room, walking through the house in his stocking feet. When he got to the front door, he opened it quietly and slipped out onto the front porch. He sat on the steps to put on his boots, took a deep breath, and walked over to the beat-up silver Honda Civic his father had given him the day he brought home a brand-new BMW. So far, so good. It wasn't until Terry was almost all the way to Prescott High that he realized he'd been shaking all over.

Heather's car was in the parking lot, nosed up against Blaze's motorcycle. Terry locked up his car and ran through the school, downstairs to Room 228.

They all looked up when he walked in. Ashley was white and pasty. She was wearing a bowling shirt with RITA AND INEZ'S BEAUTY

PARLOR embroidered across the back in red ten-ply thread.

Heather had on a pair of jeans and some kind of soft pink oversize shirt. As usual, her beauty was blinding. Blaze sat across from Heather, immune to her beauty, with his feet on the table between them. Heather kept looking at Blaze's boots in disgust.

"Crowley get here yet?" Terry asked.

Heather shook her head, produced a nail-polishing stick, and began polishing her fingernails.

"Do you *have* to do that in here?" Ashley complained. "You're smelling up the entire room with nail polish fumes. I mean, we have to be in here for four hours, you know?"

Terry scowled. It was becoming a very oppressive day. His parents' fight first thing this morning, and now Heather and Ashley were at each other. All Terry wanted to do was leave. But he couldn't leave the Yearbook Committee room until Crowley showed up to take attendance. He was trapped. It was his two worst nightmares come true: being locked in a small windowless room and being in direct contact with two people screaming at each other. Plus Blaze. Blaze was chilled out. It was like his total existence was set on cruise control. Terry felt that his own, on the other hand, was locked in at alien attack.

Ashley looked around the room, pulled a mangled copy of *Carrie* out of her bag, turned to the folded-down page corner that marked her place, and began to read.

Under his breath, Blaze started to sing all the verses of "Everybody Run, Homecoming Queen's Got a Gun." Ashley and Heather looked up, personally offended when Terry started snickering.

By the time Ms. Crowley walked in, the entire room was heated up for armed warfare. Terry slouched in his chair as Ms. Crowley dumped a stack of assorted workbooks on the worktable. She looked at Terry and smiled. He didn't smile back; he settled down to wait. Women had been smiling at him since he was four years old. It didn't mean a thing.

"Let's see what you've done since last week," Ms. Crowley began. She was wearing some kind of shirt that buttoned up to the neck. The shirt was putty-color and made her skin look green.

"Have you set up systems or anything?" she prompted. "Figured out some kind of working arrangement?"

Terry finally smiled; the woman had clearly lost all reason.

"Well," Ms. Crowley added when no one jumped up to volunteer information. "Perhaps one of you would like to update me on the status of this project." Her eyes darted around the room. "Blaze?"

"Yeah, well, I guess you could say we figured out a couple of things," Blaze assured her.

"*What* things?" Ms. Crowley's gaze bore down on them like a minesweeper. "Terry?"

Terry cleared his throat. "Of course, things

are still basically in the working stages. Right now, we're investigating a couple of approaches, but we'll have something more for you next week."

"I hope so." Under the words lurked a hidden threat. Clearly, outside of taking attendance, there was nothing here for her to do. "I'll be back to dismiss you around noon. I want to see what you've done by then. Am I making myself clear?"

"Crys-tal-line." Blaze muttered, staring at the ceiling.

"You don't have that much time to play around," Ms. Crowley warned them. "And you don't want to get into a situation where you cut it too close to the wire and don't do your best work."

Terry fidgeted. They were *only* coming up with tag lines; it wasn't like they were discovering a cure for cancer.

"I'd like to remind you that this is a serious business. No extracurricular activity, no graduation. Think about it." Ms. Crowley's cold eyes probed each of their faces in turn. Then Ms. Crowley picked up her workbooks and left.

Heather put her head in her hands. "I can't stand it."

"What's the matter, Heather Feather?" Blaze put his hands in his jacket pockets. "World too rough for you?"

But Terry had had enough. He jumped out of his seat and began pacing up and down the length of the room.

Everyone looked at him in complete surprise. Suddenly Terry realized he was in a room with people.

After a minute of complete silence, Ashley put down her book. "It's not that bad," she offered.

"What do you know?" Terry snapped, as Heather stared at him in shock. "Who are you to tell me it's not that bad?"

Ashley shrugged. "Well, hey, forget it."

"What's bugging you, Wallace?" Blaze prodded.

"Nothing. I can take care of it myself."

"I can see that." Heather, sensing that his energetic outburst wasn't going to escalate into violence, had turned sarcastic. "I hear you hit on Lisa Donnelly at Jeremy's party. Asked *her* to write the tag lines. Frankly I think that's revolting."

"You do? You think it's revolting. Well, at least I'm doing something. I haven't noticed you taking any steps to do anything around here but make alterations in your physical presence."

"What's everybody so down on me for?" Heather whined.

Waves of anger were working their way up from Terry's stomach and threatening to shoot through his head. "I gotta get out of here."

"Chill, Wallace," Blaze commanded. "There's nowhere else."

Blaze was right. As suddenly as it had come, Terry's anger left him. His head felt like it was filled with diesel fuel.

"Where do you think you're going to go?" Blaze asked softly.

The man had a point. Where was he going to go? Back home? Where his parents were undoubtedly winding up for round two? Over to Tom Sargent's? Not this early, if he was planning to spend the night. He didn't even have enough money to go driving around. He had two dollars in quarters in his pockets. Two bucks didn't buy a lot of gas.

Terry felt so unutterably lonely, he could taste it as bitterly as if he'd filled his mouth with grapefruit peel.

He looked at his knees. There was a big frayed rip in the left leg of his jeans, and his bones were poking out. Knobby bones all covered with knee hairs. Self-consciously, Terry tried to hold the rip in his pants together with his fingers. What was he going to do?

"I don't know," Ashley suggested. "We could come up with tag lines for one another. Maybe we'll, like, take off from there, and the impetus will carry us along for a while." Ashley was being stubbornly optimistic, but at least it was something. There was still Lisa, but who knew if she'd pan out in the long run? Usually women did. Usually they bailed you out. But if the whole school was talking about how he'd set Lisa up at Jeremy's party, well, Terry couldn't blame her if she let him down. It had been a shot in the dark, that's all. Desperation. Terry took a deep breath. "Heather should be 'Most Beautiful.'"

Everyone, including Heather, nodded solemnly.

"Who's writing this down?" he asked.

"I will." Heather, mellowed out by being "Most Beautiful," dug a pink felt-tip pen out of her purse and reached for a legal pad at the end of the table beside the typewriter. "And Blaze can be 'Class Rebel,' " she volunteered, as she wrote in large, round handwriting. "Anybody have any objections?"

No one seemed to.

"Of course, we could always make him 'Most Likely to Succeed,' " she needled.

"I *won't* be 'Most Likely to Succeed,' " Blaze said vehemently. " 'Most Likely to Succeed' is stupid."

"And 'Class Rebel' is intelligent?"

"It has aspects," Ashley commented.

"Terry's 'Class Flirt,' " Heather continued. "There's absolutely nobody around in his league. I mean, he'll practically hustle anything that's warm and breathing. Look at Lisa."

"What's wrong with Lisa?"

"She's not exactly the world's most raving beauty," Heather insisted. "At least by normal people's standards, okay?"

"There's all kinds of beauty," Terry said gallantly.

"Oh, I suppose we're talking about *inner* beauty? Everybody knows what good that does a person."

"Inner beauty is important," Ashley insisted. "It's not just your looks that matter to you," she continued, turning toward Heather.

"Oh, no, definitely not. I have unplumbed depths." Heather's face was flushed.

"I'll just bet you do," Blaze said nastily. Heather flushed a deeper red.

"Look, can we just continue here? What about Ashley? What are we going to call Ashley? 'Most Likely to Flake Out Permanently'?" Heather said.

"Why don't you just can it, Heather?" Blaze suggested. He looked appraisingly at Ashley for a moment or two. "Let's make Ashley 'Most Unusual.'"

"Thanks a lot," said Ashley.

"It's a compliment," Blaze protested.

"You better put up and shut up, honey." Heather was philosophical. "It's the best you're gonna get. You're just lucky you happen to be on the Yearbook Committee with the rest of us, because, I promise you, it could be a lot worse. You're not exactly white bread and Velveeta."

"Well, I think everybody else's tag line is pretty good, but I don't like mine," Ashley sulked. "It has nothing to do with me. I wish people would quit making me out to be this big weirdo. I'm not like that at all underneath."

"Here we go again with the underneath," Heather complained. "This is totally the surface we're talking about here. Which some people can't seem to get through their heads."

"You know how I feel about labeling people." Ashley fingered the cover of her paperback book.

"Yeah, you better watch it, Blaze. She's liable to get all telekinetic on you," Heather warned.

She leaned back in her chair and stretched, a gesture closely observed by both Blaze and Terry. It took her a long time.

When she was finished, she looked at them and said sweetly, "Okay, we got us, now what do we do?"

Blaze reached over and pulled last year's yearbook toward them by its cover. He flipped it open to the juniors' pages.

"What did they call the seniors last year?" Heather asked curiously.

"Who cares?"

"No, really," she protested. "Don't you think we should consider precedent here?"

"Heather, if you want to consider precedent, go right ahead. Nobody's stopping you. 'Course, I don't know if you should go throwing big words like that around. No telling what kind of trouble you could get into," Blaze said.

Heather gave Blaze an extremely dirty look. "I don't know why everybody around here thinks I'm the brainless wonder."

"If I were you, I'd consider leaving out the wonder part. And, anyway, if you think you're so incredibly brilliant, why do you go around trying to convince people you're an airhead? Generally, a person's either an airhead or not."

"Look at Marilyn Monroe," Heather argued. "Everybody thought she was an airhead, too, and she wasn't."

"She's dead," Terry said sadly.

"That's right," Blaze agreed. "So it doesn't matter a whole hell of a lot whether she's an airhead now, does it?"

Heather didn't even bother to look at Blaze. "You really are ignorant, aren't you?"

"Hey. I am what I am. You hear? I don't go around pretending I'm something I'm not just because I think it's going to help me win friends," Blaze shot back.

"None of you knows how much pressure there is in being popular." Heather dismissed them all.

"Really, who cares? There's more to life than being popular," Ashley mused aloud.

"Come on, come on," Terry said wearily. "Can we get back to it, okay? We got stuff to do here."

"Yeah, but we're not going to get it done this morning, so just quit being so demanding." Heather leaned over her page of legal paper and began to draw elaborate purple flowers in the margins.

"You aspiring to the decorative arts?" Ashley asked mildly. "Textiles, maybe?"

"What is she talking about?" Heather asked Blaze and Terry.

Blaze turned pages. "Here's John Abisimira," he offered. "What can we say about him? Anybody even know the guy?"

" 'Most Likely to Fall Asleep in Family Dynamics and Never Wake Up Again.' " Heather sneered.

"That's not fair," Ashley disagreed with Heather. "Everybody falls asleep in Family Dynamics. It's totally boring, and there's movies every period. Total Darkness. What else is anybody supposed to do?"

"Well, you know him. You come up with something."

"She already did," Terry said. "He was 'Best Arms.' "

"Oh, yeah," Blaze grinned. "Back to the body parts."

"Okay," Ashley shrugged. "Give him 'Best Connected.' "

" 'Best Connected'? What's that supposed to mean?" Terry asked.

"He's got the best connected shoulders to his body of anybody in the whole world," Ashley said dreamily. "He was lifeguard at the pool last summer."

"Better connected than Rambo?" Heather wondered out loud, busy writing.

"That's Sylvester Stallone," Terry corrected. "There's no such person as Rambo."

" 'Course, if the girl had a brain," Blaze offered, "she'd figure that out."

"Don't you think it's weird," Ashley asked, "the way Sylvester Stallone's face looks exactly the same as the Statue of Liberty? I mean, if you look at both of their faces up close, Sylvester Stallone could *be* the Statue of Liberty."

"He's way too short," Blaze said, dismissing the whole idea. "Who's next?"

"Are we really calling John Abisimira 'Best Connected'?" Heather wondered.

"Why not? If Crowley has a problem with that, she'll let us know, don't you think?"

"Patricia Adamski," Blaze read out. "Any takers for Patricia Adamski?"

" 'Most Likely to Graze on the Football Field

During Halftime,' " Heather offered.

"What's that supposed to mean?" Ashley frowned.

"What do you think? Girl's a cow."

"Heather," Ashley answered in a concerned tone. "I don't know how you come up with these awful things about people."

"I don't know why they didn't put you away at birth," Terry put in, addressing Heather.

"Don't think my mother wouldn't have liked to," Heather quipped, looking in great satisfaction at Ashley's white face. "They wouldn't let her."

Everyone looked at Heather in horror. "That's right," she insisted.

"I'm not sure that's something to be proud of," Terry said uncertainly.

"Who's proud of it? It's the truth."

"How do you know?" Ashley was curious.

"She wasn't married at the time. I was born three years before she married my father. Who knows if he was my real father. Anyway, I asked her."

"And she *told* you that?" Ashley's face was getting paler by the minute.

"Can we lay off this stuff and get on with it?" Terry begged. "What are we going to say about Patricia Adamski?"

"What can anyone say about Patricia Adamski?"

"We could say 'Best Hair,' " Ashley tried.

"What do you mean 'Best Hair'? She's one of the few women in the world who'll go bald."

"Do you always have to be so catty, Heather?"

Meanwhile Terry had been getting more and more fidgety by the minute. Finally he leaned toward the table and interrupted everyone. "I have something I want to tell you guys," he said, with the passion of someone who has to get a great deal off his chest in a hurry.

"What?"

"I promised C.S. Horstig that she could be 'Most Popular.' "

"What?" Heather was becoming greatly agitated.

"You heard me."

"C.S. Horstig is the least popular girl in the whole school. Nobody has even talked to her for two years, ever since she threw up in the school cafeteria. Everybody knows that. We can't make her 'Most Popular.' "

"Why not?" Terry demanded.

"You may as well make Ashley 'Most Popular,' " Heather grumbled.

"Ashley's 'Most Unusual'; we already agreed." Blaze was firm.

"Yeah," Heather admitted, "but C.S. Horstig can't be 'Most Popular,' anyway, because I told Suzanne Romano *she* could be 'Most Popular.' "

"You what?"

"That's right." Heather smiled condescendingly at Terry. "I told her she could be 'Most Popular' last Thursday because she gave me her pink cashmere sweater."

"No!" Ashley blinked in disbelief. "I can't believe you did that."

"Why not? She's head of Pep Club, and she's on the debating team, and her parents have

money and stuff, and she's always up for Homecoming Queen."

"Yeah. And she always loses, too. Nobody
likes her. She's bratty," Terry countered.

But Heather looked unconcerned. "Well, I can
hardly help that, can I? Anyway, I already
promised and I have to keep my word."

"What about *my* word?" Terry demanded.
"I'm the one who promised C.S."

"What'd C.S. give you?" Ashley asked. "Just
out of curiosity."

"Dire Straits tickets."

"I can't believe you guys," Blaze shook his
head. "You guys are actually taking bribes."

"It's not taking bribes," Heather protested,
glaring at Blaze.

"We can get things for you guys, too," Terry
offered. "I mean, it's no big deal."

That was all Blaze needed. He exploded.
"What makes you think that I'd take anything?
How can you guys do that? What's the matter
with you, anyway?"

"Since when did you become Mr. Innocent?"
Terry asked matter-of-factly. "We're in this
crummy situation. We're practically lepers, you
know? Way I figure it, we may as well make
something off the deal, you know?" Terry
couldn't believe he was saying this. He was
sounding just like his father. "I mean, you gotta
deal any way you can. There's always *some* way
to make things work for you."

"Besides," Heather argued, "I don't see what
difference it makes who's 'Most Popular,' anyway."

"Yeah," Terry agreed. "So let's make C.S. Most Popular."

"I already told you. We have to make Suzanne 'Most Popular' because of the cashmere sweater."

"Dire Straits tickets cost more than one cashmere sweater."

"Are you kidding me?" Heather was indignant. "What did you get?"

"Mezzanine."

"Wrong. Cashmere sweater wins."

"You guys make me sick," Blaze cut in. "That's taking bribes. We can't make either one of them 'Most Popular.' "

"Why not?"

"Because they aren't, that's why."

"Look at it this way," Terry tried to explain. "What if somebody like Liz Winfield gave me Dire Straits tickets, instead. We'd have to make her 'Most Popular,' wouldn't we?"

"Why?"

"Because she *is* 'Most Popular,' and everybody knows it," Heather argued logically.

"But" — Blaze was getting mad — "she *didn't* give you Dire Straits tickets, and the person who did isn't popular at all. It'll make us a big joke."

"We're already a big joke. Least we can do is get something out of it."

"Blaze is right," Ashley decided. "Both of you guys have to give back the stuff, and we have to make Liz Winfield 'Most Popular,' anyway. And we need to have some kind of understanding from now on."

"Like what?"

"People can't go around promising they'll let people be whoever they want. Not to mention getting paid off."

"We're not getting paid off," Terry insisted scornfully. "Think of it as an exchange of services."

"Come off it, Wallace." Blaze was disgusted. "Ashley's right. You guys can't keep going around doing this stuff."

"But," Heather whined, "people *want* to do things for me. I'm really popular at this school, and it's unbelievable the amount of people who like me. Besides, for your information . . ." — she paused and looked around at the group — "it's really wrecking my reputation hanging around with the rest of you guys. I mean, kids are actually starting to avoid me."

"What kind of friend is going to stop talking to you because you got stuck on Yearbook Committee?" Ashley demanded.

"What do *you* know?" Heather looked directly at Blaze. "I just want everyone here to know that I'm keeping that sweater."

"Fine. Keep the sweater. But no way is C.S. going to be 'Most Popular,' " Ashley said firmly. "Maybe we could go on to the next person," Ashley suggested in a tone that let everyone know she wasn't about to let Heather bother her.

"Marcia Aines," Blaze read out loud from the yearbook.

"Oh, yeah, 'Best Eyesight,' " Ashley remembered. "We could say she was 'Most Likely to Get into the Air Force.'"

"Why would we want to say that?" Blaze looked over at Ashley.

"Don't you have to have twenty-twenty eyesight to fly a plane?"

Heather dropped her pen on the table. "This is just hopeless. Hopeless. How are we going to come up with stuff for everybody? I've got better things to do."

Meanwhile Terry had phased out totally. He was worrying about Lisa Donnelly. Lisa Donnelly had to come through. If she didn't, it would be serious dead zone for all of them. This just wasn't ever going to work, what they were doing here.

When Ms. Crowley came back to dismiss them, she gave them all a detention Friday for not having done anything all morning, and after she let out the Yearbook Committee for the day, Terry drove home.

He was less than ecstatic. Now he had a Yearbook detention on top of the Yearbook Committee meeting next Saturday. Yearbook was ruining his social life. When did he have time to go out anymore?

He pulled up into his street, angled the car toward the driveway, and coasted in, parking behind the Rambler. His mother was home. When he walked in the front door, he was relieved. All quiet. No one was screaming. Conversational TV was playing softly in another room, and the washer and dryer were thudding away in the basement. Simple, safe, everyday home sounds. Terry felt himself begin to relax. He was always so jumpy whenever he was home; it was the fight or flight thing. And it was probably worse with him because he never got around to doing either.

"Mom, you home?" Terry walked down the hall toward his room.

"Some girl named Lisa called for you this morning, Terry." His mother's voice came from the bathroom where, from the sound of it, she was taking a bath.

Lisa. His hope for the future.

"And Dolores must have called about twenty times. Said it was important. She was being very persistent this morning, I must say. It was early for her, too."

Terry wandered back down the hall toward the kitchen, thinking. Maybe Dolores would help him if Lisa didn't pan out. Or maybe not. Depended on what kind of mood she was in mostly. He could count on her in a crisis, but her specialty was the more dramatic stuff. She was just a dramatic kind of girl. You didn't go to Dolores for the day-to-day practical problems. Practical was for the Lisas of the world.

Terry crashed through the chest-high louvered kitchen doors and stopped dead.

There was a big hole by the refrigerator where his father had put his fist through the wallboard. Terry skidded on spilled cereal as he walked over to the kitchen table. There were scrambled eggs stuck to the wall at the back of the stove. A frying pan lay upside down in the middle of a congealed puddle of grease underneath the cupboard. The curtains that hung on the window over the sink were sliding off the curtain rod, trailing into the gray scummy dishwater that was sitting in the sink.

Terry pulled the soggy curtains out of the sink and rehung the curtain rod. He got a broom and dustpan and swept up the cornflakes. Then he wiped the eggs off the wall and the grease off the floor, picked up the frying pan, and put it to soak in the dirty water in the kitchen sink. There wasn't anything he could do about the hole in the wall.

Terry went up to his room and put on a T-shirt and clean shirt. He called Dolores, but Dolores wasn't home. Her mother thought she might be at the mall. Terry couldn't deal with the mall. Not today. All he wanted to do was get out of here and start over. He didn't know how much longer he could live like this; never knowing what was happening at home from one minute to the next, his mother always stupidly trying to act like everything was perfectly normal when it wasn't. If she wanted to be that way, fine. But something was wrong. Dead wrong.

Terry knew that life wasn't going to be all that easy. It didn't get any easier as you got older, either. It got worse. But his parents weren't dealing in anything real. They weren't getting help. They just went along, day after day, locked into the same sick garbage. Maybe it wasn't just his parents at all. Maybe that's what people turned into when they got older.

Terry walked into his room and picked up the

receiver of his Godzilla molded telephone. He dialed Lisa's number. Then he lay back on his bed with the pillow over his face.

"Hello, Lisa?"

"It's her sister." The voice sounded very young and obnoxious. "Who's this?"

"Terry Wallace."

"*The* Terry Wallace? I didn't know Lisa knew you. How long has she known you, anyway? She never said anything."

"Can you just get Lisa?" Terry asked patiently.

"Well, hey, sure. No prob. Wait'll I tell Deenie I was talking to *the* Terry Wallace."

Terry waited interminable minutes for Lisa to get herself to the phone. "Hi, Terry."

Lisa's voice sounded warm and comfortable. "What's up?"

"I did what you asked. I cut out all the pictures." Lisa sounded apologetic. "What I think is, you should come over. Take a look and all. I don't know a lot of these people."

Terry felt like he had suddenly been saved from instant death. Lisa had come through for him. There was no reason for her to, but she had. He owed her. Lisa had unknowingly saved his life. Not all human beings were bent on the destruction of their fellow man. Terry was so grateful, he didn't know what to say to Lisa. So he didn't say anything.

After a while, Lisa cleared her throat. "Terry? Are you still there? I'm sorry if I said something wrong."

"You didn't. It's not that."

"Oh! For a minute there, I thought I did something."

"You did. But it was good."

"Oh. I have to have some help with this. I don't know what I'm doing. So, if you're not doing anything this afternoon, I thought maybe you could come over or something."

"All right. You live near Andrea Glopack, don't you?"

"Yeah. They're next door." Lisa's voice sounded suddenly flat and distant.

"Okay. Give me a few minutes; I'll be right over." Without even waiting for Lisa to answer, Terry hung up the phone and picked up his jacket. He was almost out of the bedroom when the phone rang again.

"Got that, Terry?" his mother yelled from the bathroom.

Terry picked up the phone.

"Hi, hot stuff."

"Dolores." Terry was less than pleased.

"So call me back, why don't you? I mean, it's a good thing I'm not draped over the phone waiting for you to call. My entire life could have passed me by."

"Look, Dolores." Terry felt a twinge of conscience. After all, Dolores was practically his best friend. "I gotta get out of here."

"It's bad, huh?" Dolores sounded like she was about to get all mushy and understanding. "Well, you can't take parents personally."

"That's not really it." Terry always covered up, and not even Dolores knew the full extent of how bad it was at home. "I've gotta be somewhere."

"Don't let me stop you. Who're you chasing after these days?" Terry could hear slurping noises from the other end of the line. Dolores had her Coke. She was settling in for a really long talk.

"I mean it, Dolores," he warned. ". . . And, anyway, it's not like that."

"Whoah. Defensive, aren't we? Well, how about I sit around and completely redo my world to accomodate you? Whaddya think?"

"Come on, Dolores," Terry pleaded.

"It's just, you're supposed to be my best friend. I never talk to you anymore. It's like I'm scrambled eggs now that fate has thrown you together with Heather Mercer."

"Heather Mercer? What the hell are you talking about?"

"I know men," Dolores said sagely. "Their brains are — "

"Dolores, I can't hang around and have this discussion. I told you I have to be somewhere."

"Call me later. No, better: When you get dropped flat on your face, don't even bother to call. I won't be around. I'll be the one out there saying yes to life. . . ." Dolores slammed down the phone.

Terry hung up carefully and walked down the hall.

"Did you remember to call Dolores back?" Terry's mother yelled from the bathroom. Terry groaned.

He got in the car and drove over to Lisa's house. His entire life was spent in motion. He was never in one place for any length of time. It was sick. As sick as his parents. Most people spent a lot of their time at home. They didn't spend their lives trying to stay as far *away* from home as they could get. The worst part, Terry realized, was he was starting to get used to it. It seemed that if he stopped for one single second, everything would catch up to him and roll over him like a big piece of highway equipment.

Terry was also terrified of falling asleep at night, something he never admitted to anyone. He'd rather do anything than sleep. Once he fell asleep, the dreams came. The dreams were bad enough, but not nearly as bad as lying there, unable to see what was going on around him. Being completely defenseless and unguarded. Anything could happen to a person when he was sleeping. The two best things a person could do in a world that wasn't comfortable were stay awake and be a moving target.

8

Four days later Terry began to realize he was in love. He couldn't believe how much being in love made the whole world different. Everything was so much more intense than it had been BFL. BFL was what Terry called Before Falling in Love. Before Falling in Love meant before Lisa Donnelly had rescued him from his horrible life. Ever since Lisa had volunteered to help him with the yearbook tag lines, ever since she'd really come through for him, Terry had been in love.

All day long, beautiful women walked right by him, and he didn't even notice. Beautiful women threw themselves right in front of him, and he didn't even look up. Beautiful women body-blocked him, and he didn't feel a thing. The only woman he noticed was Lisa Donnelly, and he followed her everywhere. It wasn't even hard. He had no distractions. Dolores wasn't speaking to him.

Terry knew Lisa loved him back because Terry didn't believe in unrequited love. There was no such thing. When a person loved another person, it didn't happen in a vacuum. The other person always loved back.

Terry plastered Lisa's picture all over the inside of his locker; he was getting tired of Annie Lenox, anyway. He slept with Lisa's picture underneath his pillow. It was her junior picture, and she had looked different last year, but it was still her. She had kind of a wimpy haircut last year. The bangs were too short, and the sides curled kind of funny where her perm was growing out. But her eyes were the same. Her nose and especially her mouth were the same, too. When he got time, he could color in her hair and make her look better.

Lisa had been out with him two times so far. They had gone to two movies, and the mall, but the mall didn't count as going out. Terry figured they had a lot of time to be together once Yearbook Committee was over. Lisa wasn't going anywhere for the summer. The funny thing was, lately Heather had started talking to him in the halls. To Terry's surprise, he and Heather were actually becoming friends.

But Terry's heart belonged to Lisa. He figured his bedroom window looked out over Lisa's house. Of course, it was twelve blocks away but still, before he went to bed at night, Terry would stand in his window and think about Lisa. He couldn't stand it, he loved her so much; he had never loved anyone like that in the entire world.

It was obvious Lisa was crazy about him, too.

Knowing girls, Terry could tell. For one thing, she was on a diet. Lately she'd hardly been eating anything at all whenever he was around. Terry knew the first thing girls always did when they fell in love was go on a diet.

Every time he saw her in the halls with her girl friends, Lisa would giggle and try to run into the bathroom. That was another sure sign. Terry didn't know if he would have dared to fall in love with her if he hadn't been convinced she loved him back. After all, falling in love was a big commitment. It took a lot of time to think about another person that much. And you had to stop thinking about other girls, not that that was a problem. But sometimes, in his saner moments, Terry worried.

Wednesday morning Terry was waiting at Lisa's locker. He loved to watch her walk down the hall when she didn't know he was there. She'd come walking along with a couple of her friends, laughing and talking, her hair sparkling under the fluorescent school light. When Terry saw her like that, he'd feel his stomach turn over as if a big rainbow had suddenly shot through him.

Kids streamed into school and stood in groups talking and laughing. The kid down the hall two lockers from where Terry was standing was playing his tape deck, blasting The Dead Kennedys down the halls. Four kids were dancing, bumping into other kids on the way to their lockers. And then Terry saw Lisa.

She didn't look very happy. She walked along

with her shoulders hunched in, folded into herself, jounced along by the momentum of the other kids.

"Hi, Lisa." Before she could turn around, Terry put his hands on her arms. He moved his hands to her shoulders. He was amazed at how small her shoulder bones were. It was like holding two cat skulls in his hands. "I've been looking for you all morning."

"Oh. Hi, Terry."

"What's wrong?"

"Nothing." Lisa mumbled, fiddling with her Physical Science textbook. She squinted up at him, then looked away. She opened her locker and shoved her books in, before picking through the shelves. She was getting really intense with moving things around in her locker.

"You know, Lisa, ever since knowing you, like in the last couple of days — "

"Terry?" Lisa was looking at the floor.

"Yeah?"

"I have to talk to you."

"Sure."

Lisa looked even more unsure of herself. "Soon."

"This afternoon?"

Lisa nodded. "This afternoon."

Terry grinned. "Well, all right. Where do you want to meet me?"

"I don't know. What about here?"

"Okay."

Terry put his thumb under her chin and turned her face up to kiss her. "Okay, I'll see you. You're so beautiful."

"Oh?" Lisa didn't exactly sound excited.

Terry tore through his classes for the rest of the day. Lisa wanted to talk to him about something important. He cracked his knuckles all through the *Our Land and Its People* movie, until Suzanne Moran finally turned around and told him to shut up. She also told him to find some other irritating habit that was quieter and not visually obstructive.

He was a total loss in English. From there on out, for the rest of the day, it was all downhill. By the time the day was over, Terry's brain was fried. He got to Lisa's locker in seconds flat, knocking down some glassy-eyed freshman on the way.

Lisa was standing at her locker. Waiting. She was scowling, but scowling made her look even more beautiful. She looked tortured by passion.

"Lisa?" Terry decided then and there that he would just get it over with and tell her he loved her.

"We should probably go for a walk or something," she suggested.

"What about your bus?"

"This won't take long."

Terry was disappointed.

"What's wrong with that?"

"Nothing. You want to go for a walk, we'll go for a walk, okay? You ready?"

"Yeah."

They didn't say much on their way down the hall. Mostly Terry just stared at the side of

Lisa's face. He kept his arm tightly around her shoulders.

"Do me a favor, huh?" Lisa asked.

"Sure."

"Quit staring at me like that; it makes me nervous."

"No problem." Terry shoved his hands in his pockets and watched his feet walk down the hall the rest of the way. Then he watched his hands open the door. Once outside, he put his thumbs in his belt loops and watched the parking lot.

Lisa led him around back, past the parking lot, to the Dumpsters and the incinerator, to the east wing of the school. Then she leaned up against the wall.

Lisa took a big breath. "Look, Terry, I just want you to know I'm really sorry about all of this. I don't know what else to do."

"What are you sorry about?" Terry turned to face her. He put his hands on her waist, just above her hips.

"That's just it. I keep trying to talk to you, but you just don't understand." Lisa was pulling his shirt button.

Terry smiled. She needed reassurance. "Hey, it's all right. That's what I like about our relationship, you know. We understand each other. We don't have to say things right out like other people. We just know what each other is thinking, right?"

"So what am I thinking?"

"You're trying to get around to asking me if I love you. It probably bothers you that I never said I love you. I can understand that. Girls like guys to tell them that, but, see, the thing is, before I told you anything like that I wanted to make dead sure. Now I think — "

"Terry, stop talking."

Terry stopped.

"That's not what I was thinking."

"Oh. Sorry. What is it?"

"I've been trying to tell you that we've had good times, but the thing is, I can't see you anymore."

"What?"

"And I wanted to ask you if we could still be friends."

"But we *are* friends. Last time I looked we were friends."

"That's not what I mean. I mean you have to stop hanging around my locker and all. You don't know how creepy that is."

"But I love you."

"You can't love me. Terry, I'm not interested in you," Lisa finally said in desperation. "I thought I was, but I'm not."

"Oh, I get it." Somehow Terry couldn't move his hands. They were still clamped around Lisa's waist.

"I guess I never *was* interested in you. I was just interested in the idea of being interested in you."

"I got it, okay? You don't have to keep saying it."

Terry felt as if he'd been kicked in the stomach. Waves of unhappiness washed over him until he thought he was going to suffocate. He shoved his hands into his pockets before Lisa had to pry them off her body.

"I really mean it about the friends part," Lisa said after a long silence. She kept talking; she wouldn't shut up. "See, the one thing I've really learned to like about you, Terry, is your mind. You've got this really great mind."

"Do you think you could stop talking?" Terry took one long last look at the love of his life and walked away. He could hear her starting to cry.

Terry didn't know where he was going to go. All he knew was he had to get away. He walked around the school twice, and when he circled around by the Dumpsters, Lisa was gone. He wasn't surprised. He was totally beyond surprise. But he wasn't beyond thinking because, on his second revolution around the school, he thought that he was really acting like an idiot. He figured he'd just go down to the Yearbook Committee room. He didn't want to go home, and nobody would be down there today. Blaze was serving a detention, Ashley was drifting around on some cloud, and Heather was probably home rubbing down her entire body with the loofah she'd bought. Maybe he'd try to call Dolores later, but right now he just wanted to be alone. Dolores would just say "I told you so." She wasn't really big on love.

Terry walked the length of the school and headed down the hall the back way. There was nothing alive down here. Even the girls' gym was empty. Just like his life.

Terry walked into Room 228, turned on the

light, and sank down in the green chair that was Heather's favorite. He leaned his head back, stared at the ceiling, and let his body go limp. Now all he had to do was figure out how to fall *out* of love. Supposedly, there were ways to make yourself fall out of love. Dolores had told him all about it. Terry tried to think about something he really hated a lot about Lisa. He couldn't think of anything. He wasn't too crazy about the way she ate yogurt, but he'd only seen her do it twice. She kind of ate down one side of the carton and then ate down the other.

"Are you alone? Can I come in?" Heather was standing at the door staring at him. She was probably trying to be funny.

"Hi."

"I, uh, lost my favorite makeup brush. You know the little one I use for contouring? And I thought maybe I left it in here." Heather walked in and sat down. "What's the matter with you?"

"I had a bad day, and I don't feel like seeing anybody."

"Touchy."

"Yeah."

"You look like somebody just dumped you," Heather said wisely. "And I didn't even know you were going out with anybody."

"I guess we weren't. Look, I was wrong all along. Does that make you happy?"

Heather looked at him. "Was it that Lisa person? I tried to tell you, Terry; she goes out with this college guy. Everybody knows that."

Terry put his head in his hands. "She said all this stuff."

"Like what?"

"I don't really want to talk about it."

"Look at it this way." Heather was trying to help. "Isn't it better that it happened now?"

"As opposed to when?"

"Actually, I know how you feel."

"Don't make me laugh. You've never been in love in your whole life with anybody who wasn't yourself," Terry said.

"Hey. *I* didn't break up with you."

Terry's throat began to prickle. He rubbed his eyes; some kind of mist had suddenly got in them.

Heather flounced around the room in exasperation. "Who would have figured you for falling in love?"

"Meaning?"

"Hey, you're 'Class Flirt.' You're very charming, but most people know it doesn't mean anything. Let's face it, you like women."

"What's wrong with that?" Terry asked defensively.

"Nothing. Look, I'm right; will you just admit it?"

"You're unfeeling."

Heather looked at him in surprise.

"I'm seriously depressed here, and you don't even care, do you? I wouldn't treat you like this. You're just making me feel worse."

Heather shrugged. "So empathy isn't one of my strong points."

"You're chipping off your nail polish," Terry said snidely.

Heather's face flushed. "So, what if I am?"

"I just thought you'd like to know."

"For your information, I *do* feel bad for you. You think this was easy for me? I can't believe you went and fell in love with Lisa Donnelly. You could have done a lot better. Maybe I like you, Terry. Did you ever think about that?"

"*You?*"

"You're not a bad guy when you aren't distracted." Heather took a deep breath. "I'm only telling you this because nobody else is going to, that's for sure."

"But you hate me," insisted Terry.

"I got over it, okay? You're likable. But you're always falling in love every fifteen minutes with somebody completely new."

"That's not true. The whole time I loved Lisa, the only other girl I even talked to was you. Dolores and I aren't talking anymore." Terry stared at the floor.

"Yeah. I noticed."

"I was serious about Lisa," Terry said mournfully.

"Who cares? I thought you knew *I* liked you. I mean, I've practically been throwing myself at you. I'm always hanging around places you'll show up at sooner or later. Except today. I really did lose my contouring brush."

"I guess I didn't notice."

"Well, thanks a lot," Heather said.

"I didn't mean it like that."

"How did you mean it, then?" Heather walked over toward him. Terry thought long and hard about Lisa for a couple of minutes before he realized he might be starting to fall in love again.

Then Heather kissed him. Terry realized, suddenly, that all this time he'd just *thought* he was in love with Lisa. He'd been completely wrong all along. Maybe the person he'd really been put on this Earth to love was Heather. It was an interesting possibility.

Heather

9

It was early Saturday night. Heather sat in front of the antique Sheraton mirror in the bedroom. Her mother had bought it for her several years ago, when Heather asked if she could redo her room. At the time, she hadn't exactly had Sheraton vanities and Laura Ashley wallpaper in mind, but that's what she'd got. It was a dumb bedroom, but Heather had plastered posters all over the walls, covering up most of the wallpaper. There wasn't a lot of the vanity actually visible; the mirror was ringed with tear sheets from magazines taped to the glass, and the top surface was covered with bottles, jars, and powdered rounds of color.

Heather's room was a mess. Clothes and shoes were strewn across the floor, and the closet was a tangle of fabric. "Slave of Love" was blaring out across the room from Heather's stereo.

Heather's hair was pinned back with four-inch steel clips, and she had a pink towel thrown around her neck. She studied her face for enlarged pores.

"Heather, you don't have all night. We have to be at La Ronde at eight." Mrs. Mercer stood in the door, her arms folded across her chest. She was impeccably and tastefully dressed in a cobalt-blue silk dress and the opera-length pearls Heather's stepfather had brought her from Hong Kong. "What are you wearing?"

"My sleeveless green silk shirt with a tie and my new linen blazer." Heather watched her mother's face from the mirror for signs of life.

"That sounds perfectly hideous."

"Why?"

"Clothes are supposed to enhance the person who is wearing them, Heather. They're not supposed to draw attention to themselves. I'm not going to fight you, Heather. But I do wish you would stop insisting on appearing in a costume wherever you go."

"I'm a conservative dresser, Mother. You should see what the kids at school wear."

"I don't particularly care what the kids at school wear."

"Look, Mom, I know you're nervous about tonight." Heather smeared moisturizer on her face. "Don't worry so much."

Mrs. Mercer ignored her. "I expect you to be dressed and downstairs in the hall in an hour. Wearing something sensible and appropriate." With that, she stalked off.

Heather sighed, opened the drawer in her vanity, and pulled out the shopping bag of cosmetics she'd bought with her mother's charge card this afternoon. Her mother would kill her if she knew. She'd find out soon enough, but for now, Heather didn't care. She knew her mother was nervous about tonight's dinner. Heather's stepsister worked for a major advertising company in New York and was flying in to visit for a couple of days. Chauncey Mercer always made Heather's mother crazy. Chauncey was beautiful, successful, and her father's daughter; everything Heather wasn't.

Heather knew her stepfather considered her mentally deficient compared to Chauncey. Which was fine with Heather. She figured she could get around him more easily that way. Let him think she was a dumb blonde. Heather knew how to play it, and she was a long way from dumb. Heather thought *Chauncey* was stupid.

Heather pulled on a silk camisole and dabbed her neck with perfume. Her mother would probably hate the perfume, too. She'd just have to remember to sit as far away from her mother as possible at dinner. Although, with the way her mother chain-smoked all the time, Heather doubted she could still smell anything.

With the edge of a Q-tip, Heather dabbed on undereye concealer and blended it in. The makeup man at Arpel's had told Heather to do her eyes first. Heather always did what the makeup man at Arpel's said. Not that she saw him that much. Among other things, Mrs. Mercer was not big on a lot of makeup for young girls.

Heather outlined the bottom rim of her eye with burgundy powder using a tiny slant-angled brush. Then she drew in eyeliner on the top of her eyelid. She covered her entire eyelid with white powder. White powder required another brush, flat and broad. She drew caramel-colored shadow over her eyelids, and with a fluff brush, outlined in dark-brown shadow the outside of her eyes.

She opened the bag of cosmetics and took out a brand-new bottle of foundation. The makeup man at the cosmetics counter told her she didn't really need foundation, but Heather wanted to wear it, anyway. She was convinced she needed it to cover her enlarged pores. The makeup man told her that if she had enlarged pores, he was Joan Crawford. With the other end of the Q-tip, Heather dotted her face with foundation and worked it into her skin with a silk cosmetic sponge. Then, with a big red sable brush, which she'd also bought today, Heather dusted her face with her new translucent powder.

She looked at her face critically and smiled. Chauncey Mercer would see her and weep. Chauncey considered herself so beautiful and sophisticated it was disgusting. What Chauncey Mercer was, was old. She was at least twenty-six, and she had wrinkles already. If Heather had wrinkles under her eyes and along the sides of her mouth as Chauncey did, she'd hide under her bed for the rest of her natural life.

Heather put on the navy mascara and checked out her eyelashes for clumps. Clumps were the worst. They flaked off and fell into your food. This was something not everyone understood.

Probably women all over America ate grams of flaked mascara everyday and thought nothing of it.

Heather picked up her contour brush to do her cheekbones and thought about Terry. Terry had been a real mess this morning. It was incredible. Terry, the big flirt, torn apart by some girl. He deserved it. He had the attention span of a newt when it came to women. That was something she was going to have to watch out for. Terry had wandering eyes, and Heather hated anyone's eyes to wander too far from her. She was someone of star quality. She deserved the total attention of the people around her. She *needed* the total attention, almost to survive.

It hadn't surprised her when they picked her to be "Most Beautiful." Who else was even in the running? Most of the girls at school practically put on their makeup with a palette knife. Or else they didn't bother with any at all which, in Heather's opinion, was practically the kiss of death.

Over the contour, Heather brushed on her blusher and swiped the top of her cheekbones with white highlight powder. Then, with a sable lipbrush, she put on her lipstick. The lipstick was new, too. It was red with a hint of metallic gold that Heather thought looked drop-dead with her blonde hair. When she was finished, Heather smiled. Better. Now she was cooking. Things were looking up. She'd wipe Chauncey off the map. Besides, she had an ace in the hole. If she started feeling too upset with the pressure of having this serious dinner with Chauncey, her stepfather, and her mother, she could always daydream about Terry.

Heather knew exactly what this dinner would be like — it would be like all the other dinners they'd had together. Chauncey and Mr. Mercer would talk to each other all evening, mostly about how great Chauncey was and how successful she was going to be. Then, when dessert was finished and everyone was feeling really fat, the two of them would look over at Heather and her mother as if they were total strangers who had just arrived from Duluth. Heather hated these dinners; they always gave her indigestion.

Heather pulled out her silk shirt and slid it over her head, tossing her newly highlighted (yesterday at the salon) hair out of the way. It had taken her six solid weeks of tormenting her mother to let her get a haircut at Louis's. While she was there, she had had the highlights put in. That hadn't appeared on her mother's bill yet, either. But by the time the bill came around, her mother would be in utter torment about some new thing her stepfather had done, and Heather figured she didn't have to sweat it. Life was okay if you just paid attention to timing.

The only thing that made life less than perfect for Heather Mercer was Ashley DeWitt. That girl was a problem. She wasn't as weird as she let on. Heather was on to her. Ashley DeWitt did it all for effect. Being weird was a sure thing to get attention, and Ashley had perfected it to a science. But attention was the thing Heather intended to have for herself. She had no intention of sharing it with Ashley — even on the Yearbook Committee.

Heather knew all about Ashley. But she was taking care of that one. In a couple weeks or so, Ashley would be a sniveling mess, and sniveling messes weren't attractive. A couple of more weeks and people would forget all about Ashley DeWitt, and that was about perfect timing for the Yearbook Dance. The way Heather had it figured, by the time the dance rolled around, Ashley would be yesterday's news. And no one would suspect that Heather had anything to do with it.

Heather pulled on a thigh-length silk and wool purple sweater and a pair of tapered camel-colored pants, the only pair of pants actually hanging in her closet. From the bottom of the shopping bag she dragged out the new shoes she'd bought. She couldn't resist them: They had the most incredible purple heels with multicolored rainbows on the toes. Heather slipped them on and immediately grew several inches taller than her normal height, which made her look, in her opinion, even more striking. Chauncey Mercer was about to mourn her lost youth.

"Heather!" Mrs. Mercer was screaming at her from somewhere downstairs.

"I'm ready, Mother."

"Your father is waiting in the car."

What else was new? Her stepfather was always waiting for them in the car. Let him wait;

the only one he really cared about seeing was Chauncey, anyway. Heather picked up her purse from the bed, jammed her makeup in the side pouch, and with one more glance at herself in the mirror, was out the door.

"That sweater looks very nice on you, dear," her mother said vaguely as they got in the car. Mr. Mercer looked at Heather in his rearview mirror before starting the car. He didn't say anything. But then Chauncey was the only daughter who got kind words from Mr. Mercer.

It had all been arranged that Chauncey, who was in town for some kind of business and staying at a hotel, would meet them at the restaurant. Mr. Mercer talked the entire ride over about Chauncey, while Heather tried not to listen. They pulled up at La Ronde, and a valet parked the car.

Chauncey was waiting for them at the table. Heather, having to choose between sitting next to her mother or Chauncey, picked her mother and decided to worry about the perfume issue later. Heather glared at Chauncey from across the table as Chauncey quizzed her about school. She asked dumb questions like "How do you like school?" and made stupid comments like "You really do look very nice." Chauncey herself didn't look nice despite the red Anne Klein blazer. She had big rings underneath her eyes. Her eyes themselves were kind of bloodshot. Chauncey looked like a person who could have used about three weeks of solid sleep. But even though she was a wreck, Chauncey managed to dominate the conversation and capture all her father's attention.

Heather sighed and looked around the room for cute boys. There was one sitting two tables down from them. He was practically staring at her. One of the busboys was totally gorgeous. He looked like something out of some movie about Berlin in 1931. He looked over and winked. Heather pushed out her lower lip in what she hoped looked like a French pout.

After a while, a waiter came and took their order, and Mr. Mercer made a big deal out of ordering wine for the table. The table, Heather assumed, included herself. In spite of the busboy and the boy over at the other table, this was going to be a boring dinner. Heather couldn't stand to hear about Chauncey's job much more. Heather decided she needed to visit the ladies' room. She excused herself and found the bathroom, where she washed her hands. Then she walked into the bar and watched TV for a couple of minutes, until the bartender and two men drinking Scotch started to stare at her. There weren't many places to explore in the restaurant, but Heather checked out all of them before returning to her seat. Her mother gave her a worried glance.

"Are you feeling all right, Heather?" she asked sharply.

"I'm fine, Mother." Heather put her napkin in her lap and folded her hands over it. The wine came, and they all had a glass. Heather and her mother sat silently as Mr. Mercer and

Chauncey kept talking about Chauncey's career. Right then and there, Heather decided to become a famous actress. If she were a famous actress, then her stepfather would notice her. Like the boy at the other table. He was certainly noticing her. He was practically falling off his chair and dropping his food on the floor. Heather gave him a slow smile.

Next to the table was a rigged-up waterfall contraption with lights shining on it. People had thrown an uncountable amount of pennies into the pool, but Heather was so bored she started counting the pennies. She'd got to somewhere around ten dollars in change when she suddenly realized someone was talking to her. It was Chauncey.

Heather looked at Chauncey blandly. "I'm sorry, I wasn't listening."

But that didn't stop Chauncey. "I asked you how you have been doing, Heather. You know, you are welcome to come out to New York and visit me anytime you'd like."

Heather's mother cleared her throat nervously.

"You'll really find yourself when you get to college, I think," Chauncey continued, not paying any attention to Heather's total lack of interest in the conversation. "You'll have all kinds of opportunities, and you'll meet all sorts of new people. What are you interested in, Heather?"

How was she supposed to know what she was interested in? Did she have to have her whole life planned out this second? "Nothing," she said.

Heather's mother couldn't stop herself. "Don't be so sullen, Heather."

"I'm not being sullen."

"Chauncey's interested in you."

Heather knew that Chauncey Mercer, most beautiful member of the Mercer family, was about as interested in her stepsister as she was in that fake marble fountain. "I'm sure."

They were interrupted in the middle of more lame conversation when the waiter brought their food, and interrupted again when the busboy, in an energetic outburst, brought them another basket of bread: They hadn't even touched the first one yet.

"Have you given any thought as to what you'd like to do?" Chauncey asked, raising her wineglass.

Heather looked at her own wineglass. Empty. She was only allowed one glass of wine at dinner. "I'm going to be in the movies," Heather said matter-of-factly, having just decided at the beginning of dinner.

"Well, you certainly have the face for it," Chauncey said graciously. "You have one of those faces the camera would love, I think."

"Or maybe I'll devote my life to helping lepers. Of course, we'll probably have a nuclear war or something in the meantime, and I won't have to worry about what I'm going to be."

"I suppose it's possible," Chauncey said.

"Heather is having problems finding herself,"

Mr. Mercer explained, giving Chauncey one of his looks.

"Well, she's at a difficult age." The only difficult thing about my *age*, Heather thought, glaring at Chauncey, is that it happens to coincide with this dinner.

Heather could feel her mother shifting around. She wished her mother would say something, anything. But Mrs. Mercer never said much when Chauncey was around. Heather knew Chauncey didn't think her mother was all that great, and that her father could have done better than to marry his divorced secretary, who had been a single mother with a child of seven.

"Are you interested in any young men?" Chauncey was flailing around for conversation.

"As a matter of fact, yes," Heather said, surprising herself. She was. She was interested in Terry. "He's 'Class Flirt.' "

"I beg your pardon?"

"This year. We elected him 'Class Flirt.' Of the senior class. I'm 'Most Beautiful.' "

Chauncey smiled in what Heather decided was a patronizing way.

"Chauncey was 'Most Successful,' " Mr. Mercer said, patting Chauncey's arm.

Heather looked at the two of them and began to seethe. Her stepfather had never patted her arm like that. Never looked at her like that.

"Nobody wanted to be 'Most Successful' at our school," Heather said.

"I have to admit it," Chauncey said, "I wasn't crazy about it myself."

Heather knew what Chauncey was trying to do. She was trying to win Heather over. Heather looked at her untouched plate of food. It was chicken with some weird white gunk on the top. White asparagus. Everything on her plate was white. Even the plate was white. Suddenly her food didn't seem very appetizing.

"It'll be all right, Heather." Chauncey was trying to be sympathetic. "Life gets a lot better once you get out of high school."

"You were fine in high school, too, Chauncey," Mr. Mercer said proudly.

Heather threw down her fork, and her eyes blazed. "Andy, I don't know why you made me and Mother come to this stupid dinner. I mean, what do you want us here for? We're both just in the way."

"Heather!" Mrs. Mercer was staring at Heather with a shocked look on her face. Heather was disturbing the carefully smoothed-over atmosphere her mother was always trying to maintain.

"I thought we'd do things as a family for once," Mr. Mercer said firmly.

"I'm sure. But I'm not your kid. She's your kid. The only one you want. We all know that. You've got nothing to do with me, okay. I have my own father."

"I don't want to hear another word out of you, young lady," Mr. Mercer pointed his fork at her. "We'll settle this when we get home. In the meantime, let's just have our dinner. The four of us are a family despite whether you or I like it. I want you to stop upsetting your mother. In the meantime, there's twenty-five-dollars worth of food on your plate, and the least you can do is taste it."

Heather picked up her fork and stabbed her chicken. She wished she were dead. If she lived long enough, she would be, but that didn't help her now. In the meantime, Heather thought, glaring across the table at Chauncey, that girl should file down her teeth.

Dinner plodded on, and nobody even tasted anything from anybody else's plate. Mrs. Mercer was steadily smoking her way through an entire pack of cigarettes, which made the busboy happy because he kept having to come over to the table to replace the ashtray. Chauncey noticed this.

"I think you have a secret admirer," she said to Heather.

"Chauncey has a big ad campaign coming up next month," Mr. Mercer said proudly. He avoided looking at Heather. It was as if she no longer existed.

Finally they finished eating. They drove Chauncey to her hotel and waited in the car while Heather's stepfather walked Chauncey to the elevator. Heather stared out the window.

She wished she knew something about her *own* father. She'd never seen him. He just kind of left one day as far as Heather could figure out from her mother's stories. Heather had vague memories of a man she supposed was her father, buying her balloons. And a game he must have invented where he would hold her by the wrist and ankle and spin her around in careful circles. But that was all she could dredge up out of her memory. There wasn't anything else. Maybe once she got to be famous, he'd see her in a movie. He'd recognize her. He'd come and find her. He'd be wonderful, not like her stepfather at all. They would live happily ever after.

It was something to think about.

10

On Monday morning Terry Wallace was waiting at Heather's locker. He was wearing a navy-
blue shirt, white pants, and a suit jacket with
the sleeves rolled up. He was smiling. He was
also holding a small package in his hands. He
wouldn't let Heather open her locker door until
she took the package.

"I thought about you all weekend," he whispered.

"Relax, Terry." Heather elbowed him out of
the way. "It's first thing in the morning."

"Yeah. I know. Heather, you're beautiful."

"No kidding."

Terry held out the package insistently. It was
wrapped in gold paper, and the sides were
stapled. A red bow was taped to the top of the
present with electrician's tape. Terry had ob-
viously wrapped the present himself.

"I see it, Terry." Heather could also see that
Terry thought that his present would cheer her
up. He probably thought presents always

cheered girls up. "Why are you giving this to me?"

"Because I want to make your life a living hell." Terry was running out of patience. "Open it."

Heather smiled. She took the present and carefully unwrapped it. The wrapping paper fell to the floor. "Oh, Terry. Where did you get the money for this?"

Terry smiled. "Don't worry about it." Heather could not have known that Terry had gotten the bottle of incredibly expensive perfume from Ralph Torrenao. Ralph's father was a perfume wholesaler. It had hardly cost Terry anything except negotiation time.

"But this is one of the most expensive perfumes in the whole world."

"It is?" Terry asked doubtfully.

"Well, of course. You didn't know that?"

"Not really. What does it, uh, smell like?"

Heather opened the bottle and shook perfume out onto her wrists. Then she rubbed them together and touched them to her throat.

They didn't have to wait long.

Terry sniffed and said, "That smells awful. It's not really supposed to smell like that, is it?"

Heather was disgusted. "Of course it isn't supposed to smell like this." She was trying to wipe her wrists off on her locker door and gag at the same time. She sniffed at the top of the bottle.

The smell was making Terry sick to his stomach. "What's wrong, then?"

Heather spat, "It's turned or *something*, and it's totally disgusting. What's worse, it's practically all over my body," she wailed. "Did you do this on purpose? Is this 'Pick on Heather Mercer Week'? I thought we had something going. What did you do? Stay up nights thinking of terrible ways to humiliate me?"

Heather shoved the bottle back at Terry. Perfume slopped out and spattered the front of his shirt. "All right, you've had your laugh. Just get rid of this, okay?"

Terry looked stricken. "Heather, I'm really sorry. I was just trying to do something nice for you. I wasn't trying to make fun of you. I thought you'd like it. I'm sorry if I didn't do it right."

But Heather didn't even bother to look at him. "Will you do me a favor and get out of here?"

"I didn't know," Terry pleaded.

"Get away."

Terry looked at Heather. She looked back at him. He turned to walk away and crashed into Heather's knees. Heather brushed him off like he was some kind of insect. She watched him walk down the hall with the rejected bottle of perfume to the janitor supply room. He drained the bottle. Heather got her books out and fixed her hair. Of course she liked Terry, but he should know better than to hit her with a bottle of stale perfume first thing Monday morning.

By her second class Heather was in a totally foul mood. Practically the first time in her life she was feeling badly because of something she'd done to another person. Terry had only been trying to do something nice. She hadn't seen him all morning. Usually she saw him in the halls between classes, but today he seemed to have disappeared.

Heather would rather have died than admit to anyone — especially herself — how desolate she felt. Lunch was horrible. The only lunch Heather had ever had that had been this bad was the first lunch she'd had in high school when she hadn't known anyone. She'd thrown up before school for three weeks solid because she didn't have anybody to eat lunch with.

Heather went through the line and bought a plate of leaky cottage cheese and a Diet Coke. When she got to the cashier, she couldn't find her wallet, and she had to hold up the entire line while people behind her yelled and threatened her with things worse than death. Heather considered lime Jell-O down the neck worse than death.

Finally she managed to pay for her cottage cheese and slid into a chair at a table with a single empty seat near a window. She set her cottage cheese down in front of her and let out a sigh of relief. She needed some peace after such a hellish morning.

Heather had almost started in on her cottage cheese when she realized she was sitting next to Pudgy Varley. Pudgy Varley was the leader of the Night Riders, a group of boys Heather would rather have *across* the cafeteria. Heather tried not to look at Pudgy — he wasn't especially beautiful — and the rest of his gang, in hopes she could retain a bit of tranquillity. She concentrated on her cottage cheese.

Heather was doing all right so far: The Night Riders hadn't said — or done — anything to her, and she was beginning to relax again. At least, she was until Pudgy asked to borrow a quarter.

"I don't have a quarter."

"Then give me a dollar."

"Why should I?" Heather snapped. Her lunch was fast on its way to total destruction. "What did you ever do for me?"

Pudgy Varley got up from his chair next to Heather and put his arm on her shoulder. He leaned close to her so that his forehead was almost touching hers. He had big pores. "That's not the question," he informed her coldly.

Heather lent him the dollar. It was the price for peace, she figured.

Finally they left her alone. They all got up and left the lunchroom to pillage and plunder more interesting areas of Prescott High School. Actually, the lunchroom was usually beneath the Night Riders. Generally they ate lunch in the Terminal Liquors parking lot. It was only Heather's great good luck that she'd managed to land at their table today.

Once they'd gone, the table looked like the aftermath of World War III, but at least it was empty of human beings. Heather pulled out a legal pad and sipped her Diet Coke. Yearbook had gone on for entirely too long, in Heather's opinion. Someone needed to take the Yearbook Committee in hand and, Heather decided, sitting there by herself at lunch, that no one else was going to do it, so she might as well get it over with. What they needed was a system. Heather divided the list of names that Ashley had typed out last meeting into categories, according to letters of the alphabet. That might make more sense than anything else. She'd make each person responsible for a different combination of letters of the alphabet and divide up the work.

If anybody had any questions, they could talk about it, but most of these people were self-explanatory in Heather's opinion. Like the only thing Zenon Amberon could possibly be was "Kindest to Dumb Animals." He understood them. He was a dumb animal himself.

After about twenty-five minutes, Heather was starting to feel better about life in general. She was making some headway with the Yearbook titling, so she wouldn't have to spend eternal days in the Yearbook room. She had managed to entertain herself all the way through desolation lunch period. She had even escaped the shedding of blood at the hands of the Night Riders.

Heather got up to get herself another Diet Coke. That's when she saw the two of them standing at the door of the lunchroom. Terry and Ashley. Ashley was wearing some kind of purple shroud, purple high tops, and a black felt hat pulled over her eyes. She was talking earnestly to Terry, who was slouching in the door, a half smile on his face, his hands in his pockets.

Heather was livid. So *that's* what was going on. She felt stupid for spending the entire morning feeling sorry for Terry. Like it was all her fault. Well, Terry wasn't "Class Flirt" for nothing, but Ashley was getting entirely out of hand. Ashley hadn't even given Terry time to walk into the lunchroom and notice her, Heather, sitting all alone and repentant over by the window.

Heather muttered under her breath. As far as she was concerned, the sooner Yearbook was over the better. She had never been so humiliated in her life. It was worse than watching her stepfather at dinner Saturday night, admiring Chauncey and ignoring her. Ashley DeWitt was about to get hers in spades. Nothing Heather had done so far was up to what she was about to do to that Ashley girl. Ashley was history.

Heather ripped a sheet of legal paper off her pad. She wrote the foulest, most vile things on it about Ashley she could think of. She'd just drop this little item off at Ashley's locker on her way to her next class. None of the notes Ashley had received so far even touched this one in meanness. And what was more, Heather promised herself she'd keep sending Ashley these letters.

Heather narrowed her eyes as she watched Ashley and Terry. They probably thought they looked cute together. When Terry reached over and touched Ashley's shoulder, Heather thought she was going to jump across the room and throttle them both. Right at that moment, Heather hated Terry and Ashley more than she'd hated anyone in her entire life.

The whole reason they hadn't gotten anything done on Yearbook Committee so far was because of Ashley. Ashley being vague. Nobody could get anything done with Ashley about to wig out every two seconds. Who could concentrate under those kinds of conditions? Heather thought that, later on, if she had time, she just might stop by Ms. Crowley's classroom and tell her a few things. Ashley would just have to learn the hard way. Cardinal rule number one was that nobody went around taking what Heather Mercer wanted.

Heather picked up her tray and dumped the whole thing in the garbage on her way out the back door — tray, silverware, cottage cheese, and all. She left Terry and Ashley still talking in the doorway, although what they had to talk about, Heather had no idea. She headed for the girls' bathroom, which was full of smoke, and touched up her eye makeup in the mirror. Her hand was shaking, and she could barely get her eyeliner on in a straight line.

The tardy bell rang when Heather was still in the bathroom, but she didn't care. She was late, anyway, so she might as well take her time and stop by Ashley's locker. By the time Heather got there the halls were completely deserted. Even that creep who hung out at his locker across the hall was gone. Heather folded the note into a tiny little wad, and taped it firmly to the front of the locker with a roll of Scotch tape she carried around just for that purpose. Then, smiling evilly to herself, Heather went to Home Economics.

Mrs. Tovey looked up when Heather walked into class. "Do you have a tardy slip, Heather?" she asked politely.

"No, Mrs. Tovey."

Mrs. Tovey shook her head sorrowfully. "I'm afraid I'll have to assign you a detention, dear."

Heather got two detentions from Mrs. Tovey that afternoon: one for being late to class, and another for not progressing on her apron. Someone had opened Heather's sewing box by mistake, and Mrs. Tovey had discovered that Heather was making a bikini out of her apron material. It was a good bikini, too, but Mrs. Tovey said bikinis were obscene.

Tuesday and Wednesday went by like little blurs. By Thursday, Heather hadn't seen Terry once all week except for Monday at lunch. Heather decided she didn't care one way or the other about Terry Wallace and what he did in his spare time.

By Thursday afternoon, Heather Mercer was in the best mood of her entire life. Guys had been saying thrilling things to her all day long, and during lunch, gorgeous Craig Armstrong had stopped by her table to talk to her in front of everybody in the whole lunchroom. It looked like the war between the entire world and Heather Mercer had become a cease-fire.

Life was wonderful, and Heather couldn't

understand why it couldn't be just wonderful all the time because, when it was, it topped anything else going.

Heather was practically singing with happiness as she climbed the stairs to the southwest hall crammed with noisy students on their way out. She shoved Jefferson Davis, who was busy comparing tests with Marshall Thompson in the hall, out of the way with her hip. She should have known then. Instead of Jefferson getting mad at her the way he usually did and hauling off and hitting her with his notebook, Jefferson just looked at her wordlessly and tried to talk. He looked like a really big beached fish, gasping and puffing away its life on the hot sand.

"What's with you?" Heather demanded. "Having trouble coping today?"

Jefferson reached for her shoulder and managed to stammer out a warning. "I wouldn't go over there if I were you."

"What are you talking about? This is my locker." Heather shook him off and reached for her lock. She was sorry. She should have looked. Her lock felt slimy, and when she looked down at her hand, she had to bite down on the inside of her cheek to keep from screaming. Somebody had covered her entire lock with ketchup. It oozed down the front of her locker into a bloody-looking pool on the floor. Whoever had done it must have used an entire bottle. To make it worse, taped to the front of her locker was a disgusting soft mask of a repulsive-looking female person. Crayoned down Heather's locker in gigantic red letters was the word WITCH.

Heather's face turned whiter than Jefferson's brand-new basketball shoes. Her stomach lurched. Meanwhile, people were moving away from her, shuffling slowly across to the other side of the hall, until Heather was left utterly alone in a circle of spectators with a lake of ketchup at her feet. Her mind worked overtime trying to figure out who would be mean enough and hate her enough to do something this humiliating to her. Right then and there, Heather decided that person should be ground out of the universe without mercy. Heather turned on her heel. Then the worst thing of all happened. She slipped in the ketchup and skidded across the floor, landing on her hands and knees with her chin two inches from Lester Anderson's motorcycle boots, with her books and notes scattered the entire length of the hall.

Lester let her lie there for a couple of minutes, and then he bent over her like he had all the time in the world. He pulled her up by the elbows.

"Get away from me." Heather shook him off.

"No problem." Lester removed his hands. Heather could see the laughter suppressed behind his mild expression. Furiously she stomped down the hall, picking up her notes and jamming them into her notebook. Then, without one look behind her, she flew down the hall to get the person responsible for making her the laughingstock of the entire school.

Ashley DeWitt was leaning against her locker, her books clutched to her chest, as, once again, she tried to get the combination of her lock right. Heather stormed down the hall screaming Ashley's name.

"How could you do this to me?" Heather howled. "How could you be so malicious?"

Ashley turned around in surprise and dropped her combination lock to the floor, where it promptly relocked itself.

"Ashley," Mr. Chung demanded as he appeared in his classroom door. "What is going on out here?"

"I'm not sure."

"You *are* sure." Heather flew into a rage and shoved Ashley against her locker. "What do you mean, you're not sure?"

Mr. Chung walked over to break up what appeared to be an impending fight. "Quiet down. People about to embark on an argument should pick some other place than the school halls."

"This is a school argument," Heather protested. "Ashley defaced my locker!"

"I what?"

"Don't act so innocent; I know it was you. You poured ketchup all over my locker and wrote WITCH down it in crayon."

"I did? Do I know why?" Ashley asked.

"Of course you know why! You hate me, that's why!"

"I do?"

Mr. Chung walked up to Ashley. "Do you know anything about this?"

"No! I don't." Ashley insisted. "And, anyway, I don't know why Heather is accusing me."

"But you're the only one who could have done it!" Heather said.

"Why?" Ashley asked, seeming to have only questions but no answers.

"Because I don't have any enemies."

"I can see we have a misunderstanding," Mr. Chung announced. "Would you care to explain exactly what happened?" he asked, turning to Heather.

"I told you what happened; somebody . . ." Heather stopped talking and looked at Mr. Chung. This was worse than getting ketchup on her locker. She was about to spill to a teacher.

Heather looked at Ashley, but Ashley looked confused. No matter who had done it, Heather knew she was in real trouble once she told a teacher. There was no telling what would happen to her once whoever had trashed her locker found out she'd gone and told on them.

"Heather, maybe — " Ashley began.

"Oh, shut up." Heather flounced down the hall. "You better not have had anything to do with it, because, if you did, you'll be sorry you were ever born."

When Heather got to the top of the stairwell, she turned around to look at Ashley without being too obvious. Mr. Chung had gone back into his classroom and Ashley was standing in the middle of the hall, facing the stairs, holding her combination lock in her hand. By now the halls had cleared out. Heather didn't know what she wanted to do or where she wanted to go. The only thing she knew for sure was that she didn't want to do anything public. She wanted to go home. The only trouble was, if she went home, she'd have to deal with her mother and stepfather. She'd have to spend all night sneaking around the house trying to stay out of their way.

There was only one place to go and that was shopping. Heather checked her wallet. Well, that was out. Heather had left all her mother's charge cards at home. That meant she couldn't even go over to Dynamo nails and get her nails done. Heather decided that she didn't care where she was going, she had to get out of the school. She'd go to town. She could walk around and check out the cosmetics counter at the drugstore. It was better than nothing. Worse came to worst, she could go over to Hawaii 5–0 and drown her sorrows in a nacho platter. She had enough money for a nacho platter.

Sometimes Heather didn't even know why she bothered to show up at school at all. High school was definitely not a life-affirming experience.

Heather walked out of the school the back way and headed across the football field. After five minutes of fast walking she got to the Buy-Rite. She walked in and headed over to the cosmetics counter and immediately began to feel better. She bought some soap, a bottle of henna for blondes, and purple mascara. She also bought a new cosmetics bag with rainbows and stars all over it. While Heather was standing at the checkout counter she decided that, all in all, this had been one awful week.

"Heather!"

Heather turned around. She was standing about half an inch from Terry's entire body.

No way she could pretend he'd mistaken her for someone else.

"You look bad, Heather. You look like you lost your best friend," Terry said encouragingly.

"Thanks."

"I've been looking all over for you all week."

"That's why they invented the telephone." They moved up in line, and Heather threw her merchandise on the counter.

Terry shrugged. "All right, if that's the way you want it." His eyes looked hurt.

Heather scowled at the cashier. "This hasn't been one of my more stellar weeks." She tried to convince herself she was talking to nobody in particular. "It was awful."

Heather picked up her bag by the stapled top and collected her change. "Why should I bother telling you? Are you in here for some reason or is this a strange coincidence?"

"I stopped in to get some oil. It can wait. You want to go somewhere and talk? I got a car."

"What for?"

"Heather, I miss you."

Of course, Terry was probably lying, but Heather decided she could deal with that later. Terry pushed open the door, and they walked over to his car.

Heather glared; she wasn't sure Terry could deal with what she'd been through. "You want to hear all this?"

"Yeah. Get in."

Heather got in the car. She pulled up her skirt and rubbed her knees. They still hurt from when she'd skidded across the floor at Lester Anderson's feet. The thought of it made her face burn.

"What happened to your leg?" Terry asked as he got in the car.

"I slipped in some ketchup. Somebody trashed my locker."

"Ketchup washes off, right?"

"Yeah, but it wasn't just that. They wrote WITCH all over my locker, and they stuck this horrible thing on it, like it was supposed to look like my face or something. The halls were really crowded, and I acted like an idiot," Heather finished softly.

"And?"

"Then the next thing I knew, all these people were standing around laughing at me and I slipped on the ketchup and ended up lying on the floor in front of Lester Anderson's motorcycle boots. Lester Anderson was in them at the time."

Terry slammed the car into gear and headed out toward the road. "That's kind of rough," he said sympathetically.

"Oh, what do you know about it, anyway? I don't know why I'm sitting here bothering to try to tell you about this stuff."

"What do you mean?"

Heather spread out her hands, palms up. "You don't understand."

"Who says I don't understand?"

When Heather looked at him, Terry blinked and looked away. "I got my locker trashed once," he admitted. "When I was in tenth grade, my locker was over by the cafeteria. Remember when Hellfire was around?"

"Hellfire?" Heather was thinking hard. "All I remember about them is they used to wear T-shirts with the sleeves torn out, and they tattooed their arms and pierced their ears about sixteen times."

"That's them." Terry pretended he was busy watching the road. "There were about twenty of them. Their lockers were all around mine. Twenty of them and one of me: It was hopeless. They'd just wait around for me until I came down after school. Mostly they'd just yell stuff at me, but this one day they were all standing around at the end of the hall laughing. I ignored them, like I usually tried to do, and went to my locker. I grabbed my lock, and it just about burned my hand off. See, they'd wired it up to this electrical generator. My hand was fried. I should have noticed something was wrong right away, because the bottom of the locker was kicked in and it was obvious somebody had been messing with it. So I told my homeroom teacher, and Hellfire beat me up in the parking lot in front of this girl I liked. So what I'm saying is, I know how it feels. It feels pretty bad."

They drove around for a long time, not talking. "It had to be Ashley," Heather said.

"You kidding me?"

"I saw her talking to you in the lunchroom."

"We were *talking*, Heather, not discussing how to terrorize your locker."

"Didn't look like that to me."

"Heather, what's the matter with you?"

"Nothing. Talk to whoever you want to. Makes no difference to me," Heather said sarcastically. "After all, you *are* the 'Class Flirt.'"

"You're sick, Heather."

"So I'm sick. So what? If I'm that sick, take me to the hospital," Heather fumed. "Besides, it had to be Ashley. Everyone else in this school likes me."

"It was probably someone you don't even know." Terry pulled up at a stoplight. "Where am I driving you, by the way?"

"You're driving me home, where else?"

"Well, I think Ashley's okay," said Terry.

"Oh, bore me out."

But Terry was still going on about Ashley. "She's an interesting person."

"Yeah. If you like social outcasts."

"I don't like her as much as you, you know," Terry said, turning down Heather's street.

"I don't like her at all. I hate her." Heather glared at Terry. "I thought you said something about how much you loved me, but now I don't know."

"Well, I think I *do*."

"Yeah? That's why you've spent this entire week talking to every other girl in school except me?"

"I couldn't *find* you."

"You weren't looking very hard."

"I tried to call you Monday night, but the phone was busy," Terry explained.

"It was not. Nobody was even home Monday night."

Terry shrugged. "Maybe it was Tuesday."

"Maybe. Or maybe you never bothered to call me at all."

"Look, Heather, I don't want to fight with you. I love you." Terry pulled into Heather's driveway and parked the car.

"Like hell you do." Heather got out of the car before Terry could say anything. In two seconds flat she was unlocking the door to her house.

"Heather." Terry was standing halfway out of the car, yelling across the front lawn.

"I can't hear you." Heather slammed the door and ran up to her bedroom. She threw herself on the bed and stared at the ceiling. Tears poured out of the corners of her eyes and ran down her face, but Heather ignored them. They had nothing to do with her. People like Heather Mercer didn't cry over the likes of Terry Wallace.

Why had she acted that way? She wanted to talk to Terry. She really liked him, and he *had* tried. It was just that she couldn't be second choice to him, or anyone, not even her step-father.

Heather picked at her bedspread and decided that love was totally foul.

11

Saturday morning Heather was the first person in Room 228. She was ready to work. She had perfected her system and had everything set up. She had divided up people's names in alphabetical order and split up the seniors into quarters of the alphabet, making each one of the members of the Yearbook Committee responsible for one quarter of the names. In two morning sessions, they could probably take care of the whole tagging procedure.

Blaze walked in next. He sat down at the table and picked up the sheet of paper with his name on the top. "What's this?"

"It's your list. I divided everybody into sections. When everybody does their section, I don't think it'll be that bad. I think all we really needed was some organization."

Blaze leaned back in his chair and put his hands behind his head. "Sounds good to me. I'm getting a little tired of coming in here." He looked at his list. "Hey, we can make Lester Anderson 'Most Likely to Become a Psycho-killer in Thirty Days or Less'; what do you think?"

It sounded good to Heather. Terry walked in, sat down next to Heather, and nudged her leg with his knee. "Hi, sexy."

Heather blushed. "I figured something out for us."

"You mean we can still be in love?"

"That's not what I'm talking about."

"You guys in love, huh?" Blaze commented.

"Shut up, Blaze," Heather ordered.

"She's really taking charge, isn't she?" Blaze started to drum on the table with his pen. "So, where's the old Ash?"

Ashley dragged into the room a couple of minutes later. She sat down as far away from Heather as she possibly could. Heather squirmed around uncomfortably in her seat. Heather handed Terry and Ashley their pages and explained what they should do. "You know, you guys, if you have any other ideas of what to do with this stuff, you should tell me. This just seemed to make sense, that's all."

"Looks okay to me," Terry said.

"Can we trade pages if we get stuck?" asked Ashley.

"Yeah, sure, why not?" Blaze picked up a pen and started to work. By the time Ms. Crowley came to take attendance, thanks to Heather's system, they were all hard at work. Ms. Crowley looked at them in satisfaction and left without saying anything.

"She thinks she's got us beat," Terry commented.

"Yeah, she doesn't know the half of it," Blaze said. "I'm making Cecile Dombronsky 'Most Likely to Die Without Progeny.'"

"And Les MacCradie can be 'Most Likely to Become a Newt.'" Terry read from his list.

Heather smiled and looked around the room — this was going to work. They were all actually going to get through this mess.

The Yearbook Committee room had begun to look like people were using it. Blaze had liberated another bulletin board from the storeroom and nailed it to the wall beside Ashley's asteroid poster. They had covered the board with buttons, pictures ripped out of comic books and magazines, notes to one another, cartoons, and drawings. Heather's mirror had been moved to the wall at the right of the door. Ashley hung a life-size Conan the Barbarian kite in the other corner of the ceiling, claiming it would protect them from nasty energy. Lately Ashley had been concerned about nasty energy.

In a giant explosion of generosity, Heather brought in her own personal typewriter, claiming she never used it at home anyway. They took turns typing. Ashley bought a plant and set it on a corner of the worktable after getting permission to take it out three days a week to set it in the sun so it wouldn't croak. Blaze was trying to wire up a phone for them all to use, hooking it up to the phone jack in the gym teacher's office but, so far, the field hockey coach had found the wires each time. Much to Blaze's disgust they were still unable to make calls.

"How about making Dorleen 'Best Smile'?" Heather suggested.

"Wimpy, but Crowley'll like it for sure, and it's not a body part exactly," Terry decided.

They worked for half an hour in silence, and then Heather put down her paper, took out a hand mirror, and touched up her mascara. Terry's eyes darkened as he watched her. "Do you know that I spend a good half of my conversational life watching girls fix their faces?"

"I don't doubt it."

"Heather," Terry continued, holding up his page. "Can we discuss Mark McGiver? I heard — "

"Mark McGiver gives me hives."

Ashley slammed her fist down on the table and stood up. "Will you guys please stop? You're giving me a headache."

"At least we're working." Heather stared at Ashley. It was getting to be weird-out time for Ashley. She was long overdue.

"I'm not talking about that."

"What's the matter with you, then?" Actually Heather suspected she knew what was the matter with Ashley, and she was starting, in spite of herself, to feel kind of guilty.

"Maybe I have a reason to act like this, did you ever think about that?"

Heather shrugged. "Maybe you've flipped out."

"It's better than being mean!" Ashley shot back.

"Who says I'm mean?" Heather had to find out exactly how much Ashley knew.

Ashley walked around the table and grabbed for her purse. The shoulder strap got stuck on the corner of the chair, and she tried to pull it off. It loosened with the first tug, but Ashley had tugged too hard. Her purse went flying across the room and crashed into the corner opposite the door, its contents skidding across the floor.

Blaze sighed, got up, and started to help Ashley pick her things up from the floor and stuff them back into her bag. "You got enough junk in here to survive the bomb. Hey, what's this?"

"Put that back!"

"Where? You want it in your bag or back on the floor?" Blaze started to investigate the contents of the package Ashley tied together with kite string.

"Please leave it alone." Ashley was tugging at his arms.

But Blaze was pulling the pages in the packet free and opening them up to read. Although the letters were scrunched, folded, and tied together there were still enough in the packet to make a small pile.

"Please?" Ashley was desperate.

"If Ashley doesn't want you to read that, you shouldn't read it," Heather said, equally desperate.

"I watch you all the time," Blaze read. "The worst person on the whole Yearbook Committee is you." He wadded up the note and threw it on the floor before unwrapping another one. "I've been following you for a whole week now.

147

I was watching your house when your mother was gone last week."

Some of the notes were written in black marker; others were taped together using cut-out letters from newspapers and magazines. Blaze read through the whole pile, throwing each message down on the floor when he finished. Ashley picked them up again. Finally Blaze looked at her and said, "Will you put those things down? Why are you keeping them?"

Ashley blinked and looked away. "I don't know."

Heather swallowed hard. How could she have known Ashley would walk around collecting the damn things like they were seashells? Heather wished she could take them back right now. What if everybody found out she was the one who'd sent them? Heather grabbed the crumpled bits of paper. "Throw them out," she ordered.

Ashley slumped in her chair. "It's a lot of work for one person to go to, just to make me miserable."

Blaze wadded up a handful and stuffed them into the pockets of his leather jacket. "One thing's for sure. You're not going to carry that junk around in your purse anymore. If you can't throw them away, I will. Another thing is, we're going to find out who's doing it, and then we'll get them. It's a real creep city thing to do to another person. Whoever did it is dead meat. I promise you that."

"Maybe it was a mistake," Heather ventured, but nobody was listening to her.

"You can't do anything to them." Ashley hung her head.

"You wanna bet? You wait. They're dead meat, hear me?" Blaze promised.

Ashley was glowering. "I can take care of myself, you know."

"You're doing a great job."

"I don't want you going around trying to protect me."

"Who said I was protecting you?" Blaze demanded.

"I thought that's what you meant."

"I just can't believe somebody's been doing that to you," Terry said. "It's worse than what happened to Heather."

"Yeah. . . ." Heather's voice trailed off. "Listen, let's get back to work, okay? Wouldn't it be great if this time when Crowley comes around, we could show her we have everything under control? Maybe she'd even leave us alone and stop treating us like juveniles."

"Don't count on it," Blaze warned.

Heather shrugged. "Okay, be like that. Thing is, this yearbook stuff has become a severe drain on my really good energy. It's like runoff, you know?" Heather tried to finesse the situation, but the real reason she didn't want Yearbook Committee to continue a minute longer than it had to was that she was afraid Ashley was on to her. If she hadn't already figured it out, she would soon. Heather didn't know if she wanted to be around when that happened. Especially since lately Blaze and Ashley seemed to be getting pretty tight.

The thing to do was get the whole job over with as soon as possible and clear out. School was almost over. Chances were, she'd never see Ashley again in her entire life after high school. If she could just get through the next couple of weeks without anybody finding out, she'd be okay.

But Heather's palms were sweating. It wasn't going to be easy covering up, when the four of them had to spend so much time shut up together in the tiny airless room downstairs by the furnace . . . the furnace that was beating loudly — and getting louder all the time — like Heather's guilty heart. It wasn't sending the hate notes that Heather felt guilty about. It was getting caught. She had let passion run away with her, and there was no excuse for that. She should have been a whole lot smarter.

Blaze

12

"But I still don't think it's fair, and *my* idea is more considerate," Ashley said.

Ms. Crowley looked at Ashley over the top of the typewritten sheets of tag lines that Heather had handed her as she came by to dismiss them.

Blaze stretched his legs out in front of him and pushed the sleeves of his leather jacket past his elbows. It was getting hot in Room 228.

"What would you like to suggest, Ashley?" Ms. Crowley was being sarcastic.

"I don't know." Ashley thought a minute. Blaze watched her think. He wished he could figure out why he liked Ashley. Blaze had to admit that, despite everything, Ashley did tend to take "Most Unusual" a bit too far. Like to the outer limits.

"Well, how do the rest of you feel about Ashley's idea?" Ms. Crowley asked.

The rest of them didn't have anything to say. They'd given up trying to talk Ashley out of her idea a long time ago. Ashley was not only weird, she was stubborn. And, Blaze decided, ever since she'd been getting those hate notes, she had turned even weirder.

"I think we should ask people what their fantasy for themselves in the future is," Ashley said. "It's interesting, and it isn't hurtful."

Blaze groaned. If she thought he was going to walk around school asking people their fantasies, she had another thing coming. Like, what was the girl on?

Ms. Crowley considered Ashley's suggestion. "Well, okay," she allowed. "If you can get your information together quickly, we can include people's future fantasies. Have you thought about the dance?"

Groans again. *Nobody* had thought about the dance.

"You just might give it some time," Ms. Crowley said, winding down. "Anything else?"

"I don't think so," Heather supplied, before Ashley could come up with any more bright ideas.

"Well, all right. I'll see you next time." Ms. Crowley allowed herself to give them a small smile straight from her eyes. Blaze thought the whole idea of Ms. Crowley smiling in the first place was disgusting. It was too out of character.

Ms. Crowley dismissed them from Yearbook Committee. Blaze sat at the table and watched Heather complain.

"Dipbrain!" she hissed at Ashley.

"I never did anything."

"What do you mean, you never *did* anything? What's this future fantasy bit? Now you got us all this extra work."

"I did not!" Ashley said indignantly. "If you don't want to help, I'll do it myself."

"Good. Do it yourself. Come down here every day during the week, then," Heather said, picking up her bag.

"I probably will."

"Work late at night after school by yourself, all alone with nobody around?" Heather questioned.

"I might," Ashley said uncertainly.

"I mean, I hope the ghost gets you." Heather's eyes glittered.

"What ghost?" Ashley looked at Heather, trying to hide her horror.

Heather leaned back against the wall and picked at the edge of Ashley's asteroid poster with her fingernail. "The headless linebacker who comes out of the furnace room to haunt the girls' gym every night."

"The furnace room?" Ashley jabbed her finger in the direction of the wall closest to the furnace.

"You bet. He walks right up to the door, and people can hear this horrible moaning and tapping and everything. When they open the door and look out, all they ever see is this headless body running down the hall; this neck with no head at all — just this thing running down the hall and trying to break down the door. It's the ghost linebacker," Heather finished.

"They see that?" Ashley asked.

"That's the dumbest thing I ever heard," Blaze said finally. "What are you trying to do, anyway, Heather, scare the girl?"

But Heather shot Ashley such a blatantly hostile expression that Blaze almost wished he could have choked back his words. It seemed to him that Heather was trying to do *exactly* that.

Blaze sat at the worktable with his hands crossed over his chest, one leg up on the chair opposite him, watching Terry and Heather leave. Heather and Terry, Blaze suddenly realized, were very social people. Blaze had never had much luck with social people. People weren't his favorite thing. For instance, any animal at all was better than any person. And look what people did to animals. Animals could be depended upon. People weren't like that. People were always doing bizarre stuff. Like, for instance, Heather. That look she'd given Ashley was truly bizarre.

Blaze thought about his future fantasy. He didn't usually think about the future, but when he did, he figured he'd do something in his life that didn't have much to do with people. Like being a forest ranger. He could sit on top of a fire lookout tower for the rest of his life and never have to see another human being.

Blaze shoved his chair away from the table and stood up. Ashley was having some trouble. She was shaking, having a hard time getting her notebooks together in a big pile. Every time she got them stacked up, something would fall off the pile and she'd have to start all over again.

"Hey," Blaze interrupted her. "You okay?"

"Yes," she answered timidly.

"You don't look okay. I mean, you look like you're going to cry."

"Well, I'm not!" Ashley said more definitely.

What else could he do? He'd tried. Blaze shrugged. "Want a ride anywhere?"

Ashley's lower lip was trembling. "I don't think so."

"Are you sure?"

"I *said* I don't think so!"

Blaze put his hands up in front of him, warding her off. "Okay, okay. All I was trying to do was help you out."

"You can't help me out. Nobody can," Ashley said despondently.

"I don't believe that," Blaze said.

"And, anyway, what makes you think I'd take help from someone who invaded my privacy?"

"Who invaded your privacy?"

"You pulled out all those notes and read them out loud to everybody in the whole room. How am I supposed to face Heather and Terry now that they know somebody's been sending me hate mail? I'm sure they think I deserve it."

Blaze tried to put his arm around Ashley's shoulder, but she shrugged him off. "Ashley, forget it. All I was doing was trying to help you forget about it."

"How? Maybe I *can't* forget it. Did you ever think about that? Did you?"

"Hey, listen. I'm trying to apologize here, okay? Pay attention and read my lips. I'm sorry."

But Ashley was in no mood to listen to anything. She hugged her notebooks to her chest and swept out of the door.

Blaze stared after her for a couple of minutes. Ashley was a very stubborn person. Well, if that's how she wanted it to be, there wasn't a lot he could do about it. The girl was too sensitive to live. She needed about four more layers of skin between her and the real world.

"If you want to talk," Blaze yelled down the hall after her, "you know where I am!"

"I don't want to talk!" Ashley hollered back.

"Sure you don't want a ride home?" Blaze wouldn't have minded talking to Mrs. DeWitt some more, actually. What he didn't understand was how Ashley could have a mother like that and act like she did. Blaze thought Mrs. DeWitt was a very courageous person. Ashley could really be a wimp.

"No!" Ashley yelled at Blaze. "I just want to be left alone."

Blaze shrugged. He shoved his hands in his pockets and walked out of the school the back way. There wasn't a whole lot more he could do about Ashley. The girl seemed determined to be miserable. He unlocked his bike and shot off in a cloud of dust, heading over to the reservoir. It was a brilliant day. The air was perfect. Suddenly Blaze felt a deep, wild happiness building in his chest. No matter how bad things got, everything always made sense again once he got on his bike. That's when Blaze would realize that things were never that bad. Everything was always changing.

That's why Blaze liked the reservoir. It was always changing, too. The water's surface in the reservoir never looked the same two days in a row. Sometimes it was so clear, you could see right down to the bottom. Other times it was hazy with creeping mist and fog. Especially early Sunday mornings when Blaze rode to work at Mackenzie's Sunoco station.

Blaze had to get up incredibly early for his morning shift at the gas station. Since Year-book Committee, he worked the Sunday five-A.M.-to-one-P.M. shift. If he got lucky, he'd get the afternoon shift as well. Blaze never cared how tired he was by the end of a double shift; he didn't care if he was seeing quadruple. It was worth it for the money. Working at the gas station made a lot more sense to Blaze than hanging around after school doing some kind of extracurricular activity. Working at the gas station was real life. Thinking up tag lines for members of the senior class was, as far as Blaze could figure, totally beat.

Early the next morning Blaze got up when his alarm went off. He hadn't seen anything of Ashley since she'd stormed off after Yearbook Committee. Blaze put on a black T-shirt and jeans. He'd throw on the official Sunoco shirt once he got to the station. No one in the whole house was up yet, and Blaze walked down the back stairs around the side of the house to the garage. Birds were singing in the morning darkness.

Blaze pulled the tarp off his bike and strapped on his helmet. Then he opened the garage, wheeled his bike down the driveway, and jump-started it, heading toward Route 80 and the Sunoco station.

When Blaze pulled up at the station, he looked around for Tommy. Tommy was four years older than Blaze. He was sitting in the office with Ammo, the gas station dog. Ammo ate out of a hubcap and had deformed feet like every gas station dog Blaze had ever seen. But he was faithful to his friends and mean to strangers, and the Sunoco station hadn't been robbed once during Ammo's reign.

Tommy was listening to weird music. He brought in his weird music tapes every night, and when it wasn't busy, he rigged his tape deck up to the outside speakers and broadcast across the gas station lot with running commentary between cuts. Blaze didn't mind it, though; in fact, he really liked it. Tommy was one of those people who wasn't afraid to be who he was. That feeling rubbed off on Blaze; he felt free to be himself around Tommy.

Blaze got himself a cup of dispenser coffee and a Coke and sat down at the office desk opposite Tommy to wake up. The desk was covered with grease. Ammo walked over to Blaze and put his head in Blaze's lap, staring up at him with devotion. Blaze rubbed Ammo's ears. "What's happening?"

Tommy shrugged. "Busy night."

"Yeah, I can see that."

"Lots of action down at Barrio Pete's. Guess there was a big fight around two-thirty. Smashed cars, cops, everything. You should have been around last night, Blaze — lots of girls in and out." Tommy smiled. "It's going to be a good summer. You working here this summer?"

Blaze shrugged and looked out across the highway.

"Mackenzie might give you more hours if you talk to him."

"Yeah." Blaze took a sip of coffee and settled into a comfortable silence.

"What are you going to do the last big summer before you leave for good?" Tommy asked. He wasn't being malicious, he was just naturally curious. Besides, Tommy liked Blaze.

"I don't know." Blaze had no idea what he wanted to do with his life in general.

"You should go somewhere maybe."

Blaze grunted. The coffee cup felt warm in his hands, and the Sunoco office seemed like a stopgap to an uncertain future.

"Mackenzie come by last night?" Blaze asked.

"No. Called in. He said to put the money in the safe."

"Yeah, okay. You want me to do a count at the end of my shift?"

"I don't care. Mackenzie would probably appreciate it. Although, I don't think you're going to have too much business in and out until later. Sundays have been kind of slow lately."

"So, what are *you* doing this summer, man?" Blaze asked Tommy.

"I don't know, but I have to do something. Otherwise I'll be stuck in this town for the rest of my life."

"Nobody gets stuck in towns for the rest of their lives anymore," Blaze argued; he knew he wouldn't, anyway. Even if he were undecided about the future, Blaze knew he wasn't about to keep living in Ennisclare Park.

"You gonna get married to Janie?" Blaze smiled in spite of himself. Blaze hardly ever smiled, but the thought of Tommy and Janie together restored his faith in humanity every time.

"Yeah. I guess so." Tommy shoved his hands in his pockets and started pacing the over-heated office. "Janie's been worried about me lately, and I don't know what to do about it."

Blaze nodded. He figured that's really how he'd gotten to know about love, listening to Tommy rhapsodizing about Janie for an entire year. In fact, he never would have been able to sort out his feelings for Ashley if he hadn't listened to all of Tommy's Janie-obsessed conversations.

"She wants to go away, you know?" Tommy seemed baffled. "She wants to move to the West Coast some days. Other days she wants to go to Europe. The girl doesn't know what she wants. What she doesn't understand is that all I want is *her*. I can't imagine her not being there, you know? It would be like ripping out my stomach." Tommy hit the office desk with his fist. "You tell her that, and she just looks at you with her soft eyes, and she says, 'That's not very romantic, Tommy. I like Hawaii. Hawaii's romantic. Let's go to Hawaii.' Women!" Tommy looked around the office in desolation.

Blaze knew it would work out for Tommy; he had someone he didn't have to pretend around, and that would keep them together. Blaze wished he had the same — at school everyone thought he was too tough, and at home he was the "quiet one." But Blaze believed that maybe Ashley was beginning to understand.

"I heard you were sort of hanging out with that lady artist's daughter," Tommy said suddenly.

"Who told you that?"

Tommy's eyes were dancing. "Let me see. Mackenzie? Could have been Mackenzie. He said he saw you ride by the DeWitts', staring up at the house the whole time. Didn't even recognize his truck, he said. Mackenzie said he came by there again a couple of hours later, and there you were again, riding by that house with this starstruck look in your eyes." Tommy grabbed his stomach and bent over, he was laughing so hard.

"How's Mackenzie supposed to see my eyes with my helmet on?"

"Maybe they were bugging out of your face or something. How would I know? I'm just telling you what Mackenzie said."

"I don't see what business it is of his," Blaze said.

"Aw, come on, Blaze, he likes you. I like you, too. Strange as it is, with you working here. I mean, I don't know why you even bother, living in Ennisclare Park and all. But you're all right, no foolin'. Hey, listen, I'm off. You got your first customer. See you around."

"Take it easy." Blaze walked out to the pumps and watched Tommy drive off. He checked the oil, pumped in a full tank, and took the money. It was a regular customer. One of the nurses at the hospital who worked the Sunday-morning shift. Drove a Saab. She winked at Blaze. She never talked much, but she smiled a lot.

Blaze felt good. He liked working the Sunoco station alone. Ammo went on his rounds with him, and when Blaze was done, he checked out the garage to see what cars Mackenzie was working on.

Blaze had started working for Mackenzie just after he'd got his bike. Mackenzie had been having a slow day, and he'd done some work on Blaze's bike free. A couple of weeks after that, he asked Blaze if he wanted a job. Mackenzie needed a part-timer for the weekends, and Blaze had been working for Mackenzie ever since. Sometimes Blaze thought it was the only part of his life that made any sense, the only part where he recognized himself.

People drove up, you serviced their cars, they paid you and drove off. Simple. When it wasn't busy, you could do almost anything. Only occasionally did the time drag. Sometimes people would stop by to hang out and talk, and Blaze didn't need to put on any show for them. After all, they were just strangers.

Blaze's shift passed lazily. By the time Mackenzie showed up at one, Blaze was in a good mood.

13

Blaze rode home on his motorcycle and hit the driveway. His father's car was gone. Blaze did a revolving wheelie before he put his bike away. He went up to his room to change and was just about to go down to the kitchen to get something to eat when he heard the doorbell ring.

"Blaze, can you get that?" His mother yelled from the kitchen.

Blaze ran down the stairs and opened the door. He almost slammed it shut again. Ashley was fidgeting on the front step. "I came over to see you. You didn't tell me you live in Ennisclare Park." She looked at him accusingly.

"Well, you didn't ask," Blaze said uncomfortably.

Ashley stood on the doorstep. She hadn't believed the address she'd gotten from the phonebook and now, with the "Class Rebel" standing in the doorway of a five-hundred-thousand-dollar house, she was in a state of advanced shock.

An eight-year-old girl, wearing jeans, a leotard, and leg warmers bounded into the hall. Blaze's sister regarded Ashley solemnly.

"Corin?" a voice called.

Corin looked at her brother a moment before turning her head and shouting, "Yeah, Mom?"

"Who is it?"

"I don't know. Some girl to see Blaze."

"Well, ask her in."

Corin shoved Blaze aside and pushed the door wide open with her foot. "Come in, then," she offered. Corin poked Blaze in the ribs with her elbow. "I can't believe you made her stand out there all that time."

Ashley stepped inside and looked around. "This is like walking into *Architectural Digest*," she said in awe as she followed Corin into the kitchen.

The kitchen in Blaze's house was a cheerful, gigantic cavern. The floor was red and white tile. There were navy chintz curtains on the windows, an antique oak table in the middle of the room with a typewriter and a pile of papers at one end, six chairs, and a baby at the other. The counters were clean and lined with every kitchen appliance ever invented.

Ashley had never seen so much machinery in one place. "Nice," she said. She was acting like someone who'd just stumbled onto King Tut's tomb and was a little afraid of the curse.

Blaze's little brother sat at the table in his high chair, banging his spoon against everything within his reach as a quick, fox-haired woman with a face as clean as her countertops hustled energetically around the kitchen. "Ashley, this is my mother," Blaze mumbled.

"Have a seat," the woman suggested. "I'm Eileen Conrad." She shoved a glass of milk and a plate of cookies in front of Ashley. "I'm afraid I didn't catch your name."

Blaze sat down at the table and watched Ashley looking around in shock. He wished his mother would just stop talking. He wished Ashley hadn't come over. But then, maybe this was his chance to stop pretending.

"I can't believe this is where you live," Ashley whispered as Blaze's mother washed baking dishes in the sink. "It's like being on the set of *The Brady Bunch.* I mean, it's so completely wholesome. You never mentioned you had a house like this."

"I'd love to sit down and talk with you, but I'm afraid I can't," Mrs. Conrad continued on an entirely different conversational track. "I have to get this recipe for Quik-Whip pie finished, tested, and sent to the company by nine o'clock tonight. I'm a bit under the gun with this deadline. They never can decide what they want until the last minute, and then it's just too late and always a rush."

Ashley stared at the plate of untouched cookies, and Mrs. Conrad, looking over her shoulder, smiled. "Go ahead and have one. I'm sure you've had them a million times before."

"Yeah." Corin came into the kitchen and sat down at the table beside Blaze. "It's the recipe on the back of the Stone Field Farms Rolled Oats box. Mom invented it for them. That's her job."

"What?" Ashley was trying very hard to get this straight.

"Mom makes up recipes for people." When Ashley still looked confused, Corin reached over, grabbed a cookie, and elaborated with her mouth full. "She invents recipes for, like, peanut butter freezer pops, Quik-Whip, and mushroom soup casseroles, frozen french-cut string beans, and microwave soufflés."

"Corin, stop talking with your mouth full. You're getting crumbs all over everything," Blaze ordered.

"Sorry." Corin sheepishly shoved pieces of cookie back into her mouth. "Hey, are you sure my brother told you to come over today? He seems kind of surprised to see you."

Ashley blushed. At first she'd just wanted to see Blaze, but when she'd found his address she couldn't believe it. Now she didn't know what to think, let alone how to act.

"Why don't you and Blaze go and use the VCR?" Mrs. Conrad suggested. "Brett's in his room, so he isn't using it. It's wonderful to know that Blaze has friends at school. We always assumed he was a real loner. The only thing we know for sure is that he's actually the most creative one."

Blaze winced.

"Blaze is going to get mad at you for saying all that stuff, Mom," Corin warned. "Anyway, *I'm* the creative one."

"That's true, dear. You are," Mrs. Conrad said to Corin. "But not in the same way. You're very creative in your pictures."

She turned toward Ashley. "Blaze makes up stories. You know, after a while, he can have you so convinced you almost think you're in another world."

"I know the feeling," Ashley volunteered. "This is really creepy," she said to Blaze under her breath. "You don't look like you live in this house at all. You look like you're here to do some repair work on the blender or something."

"I really like your boots," Corin said, diving underneath the table to get a better look at Ashley's ankle boots. "I wanted some exactly like that, but when my mother took me out shoe-shopping in September, we couldn't find any."

"Look, I know I probably shouldn't have come over." Blaze knew what Ashley was trying to explain to him. "I'm really sorry." Ashley was looking even more miserable than usual.

"Have a cookie, darling," Mrs. Conrad offered.

"You told me to let you know if I needed anything, but I didn't mean to interrupt you. Maybe the best thing I can do is go home or something," Ashley finished.

"Forget it, you're here now, right?" Blaze looked at her.

"What I'm trying to say is, I don't have to stay."

"You can stay. It doesn't really matter now. But if you say anything about this at school,

I promise I'll hunt you down and kill you. I don't think anyone else would understand."

"Blaze," his mother said, turning from the Cuisinart. "That's no way to talk to a perfectly nice girl. What's the matter with you? You weren't brought up to act like that."

Meanwhile, Corin was leaning across the table chewing oatmeal cookies and watching the two of them closely as both Ashley and Blaze tried to ignore her.

"Look, Blaze," Ashley said, leaning over and touching Blaze lightly on the shoulder. "I understand; really I do."

"Don't do that," Corin warned, matter-of-factly.

"Do what?"

"Touch him on the arm like that. Blaze hates to have people touching him, especially when they're girls."

"Just can it, Corin, or I'll use you in Mom's recipe for instant pâté-loaf. Shouldn't you be at modern dance or something?"

"Cranky or what!" Corin shot back. "For your information, Mom's driving me to class when she's done. Unless *you* want to."

"I can't now; Ashley's here."

"I'll just be a moment, Corin," Mrs. Conrad called. "Why don't you come over here and help me with the pie and leave Blaze and Ashley alone."

"I *hate* Quik-Whip pies!" Corin said, stomping out of the room. " 'Specially since you make one about every two days."

"She doesn't really mean it," Mrs. Conrad

explained. "She's just at that stage. Let me microwave this crust, and I'll get her out of your hair."

Blaze nodded his head and gestured for Ashley to follow him. He led her through the downstairs hall to one of the TV rooms. They had three. Plus two formal living rooms and a rec room. Blaze made sure Ashley didn't see any more of the house than he had to show her.

Meanwhile, Ashley was acting as if Blaze was a stranger. She walked by the sofa a couple of times without sitting down and finally settled in a wing chair by the window. She was only there for a minute. She was up again, rolling her hands in the bottom of her sweater, looking uncomfortable.

"You want to relax, Ashley?" Blaze walked over to the stack of videotapes and began to sort through them. "What do you want to watch: *Night of the Comet, Escape from New York,* or *Teenagers from Hell?*"

"There's no such movie as *Teenagers from Hell.*"

"Just testing."

Finally Ashley sat down on the couch. She said uncomfortably, "How could you lie to us, Blaze?"

"Who lied?"

"You told us you were this blue-collar kid. Your father was a trucker. I mean, I thought you lived in a trailer park."

"I never *told* you anything."

Blaze looked at her hard. "Look," he began, "I didn't tell you *what* you should believe. All

I did was come to school every day. I rode my bike, and I wore my jeans. So if you thought I was some kind of James Dean who gets pistol-whipped by his dad at night, well, that's not my fault."

"Why did you let us believe it?"

"Maybe I thought it was a better version of reality," he said, staring across the room. "What you have to understand is that I'm not like this house, this neighborhood, or these appliances. I didn't ask to be born *here*, and it's hard to escape it even though I want to."

Blaze put his arm around the back of the sofa. He could feel his arm hairs touching the back of Ashley's head.

Ashley swallowed hard and tried a different conversational tact. "The hates notes are really starting to bother me."

Blaze moved his arm a fraction of an inch closer to Ashley's head. He could feel her skull radiating heat up into the crook of his arm.

"I know they shouldn't, but they do."

"I'm going to find out who's doing it. I think it stinks," Blaze said.

"What did you say?" Ashley was trying to keep her voice normal.

"I'm going to find out, and I'm going to help you because I care about you." Blaze continued, "I think you're really pretty. And you're smart. And you care about people. You don't admit it, but you do. It's not really your fault if you have weird ways of showing it. The other thing is, I think you really have a good personality."

"I do?"

"Well, it isn't perfect. You do get vague, Ashley. But it's a good personality." Blaze nodded. "Yeah."

Ashley seemed to have frozen beside him. It was like she was hardly even breathing.

"Ashley?"

Ashley didn't answer. She was somewhere else.

"See? That's just what I mean. Just the kind of stuff I'm talking about here. Now you're off somewhere."

"No, I'm not. I'm right here, Blaze. I'm thinking. I got another note today." Ashley said. "They sent it to my house."

Blaze sat straight up. "Why didn't you say so?"

"You didn't ask."

"I know, but you're supposed to tell me these things, Ashley."

Ashley pulled a wadded up piece of paper out of her pocket. It had puckers on it. They looked like tear marks.

Blaze grabbed the note and uncrumpled it.

"Don't read it out loud, okay?" Ashley put her hands over her ears.

Blaze spread the note across his knees. There was a picture of a stick-figure girl in a box with a pair of scissors through her heart. "Nobody will ever love you in your whole life so you might as well get used to it now. You are ugly. You are too weird to live. I'll make you die."

Ashley was watching the video, but her eyes weren't moving. She was crying. Tears were dripping down the side of her face.

Blaze hugged her right up against him. She fit perfectly in his arm. "It's all right, Ashley."

"It isn't. I never do anything right."

"That's not it," Blaze corrected. "It's not that you never do anything right. You want to know what it really is?"

"What?"

"You're a very vague person."

"I don't try to be," Ashley whimpered.

They sat in silence, and eventually Ashley stopped crying. Blaze swallowed hard. He may as well tell her now; it was now or never.

"I had a girl friend once," Blaze admitted, never taking his eyes off the TV screen.

"Oh?"

"We used to go out. That was before we moved here."

"I get it. She writes you letters," Ashley prompted. "So you can't get involved with other people."

"Shut up," Blaze ordered. "That's not it at all."

"I'm sorry. You must miss her."

Blaze took another deep breath. "Something happened to her."

"Like what?"

"She was in this accident. My friend at the time, Joey Santor, he and this girl I'm talking about were at a party drinking and stuff. He said he'd drive her home and all, but the thing was, on the way home she and Joey stopped to go swimming in this lake and she . . . drowned." In spite of himself, Blaze felt his voice catch.

Ashley didn't say anything. They watched the video. Blaze's brother was practicing his guitar down the hall. The afternoon seemed to stop abruptly right there.

"And she died, like I said." Blaze wished he could just shut up. He didn't seem to be able to. "But Joey, well, Joey just walked away from the whole thing. Nothing happened to him at all. Nothing. Joey was my friend, and I'm glad he didn't die, but I didn't love him . . . you know? I loved her." Blaze stubbornly refused to look at Ashley.

"You don't remind me of her at all. You're not anything like her except for one thing. See, the whole point of my telling you all about this is, she was vague, too. Like you. And I always kept thinking, maybe if she hadn't been so vague, if she'd been paying attention . . . I don't know." Blaze rubbed his fists on his jeans as the blue light from the TV flickered across his face.

"I'm not vague," Ashley insisted.

"Look. It's because you're the way you are that you get these hate notes. People dump on you. You can't let that happen. You have to pay attention."

"Are you saying it's all my fault? Is that what you're saying?"

"It's your fault you kept all those letters tied up in a little pile. What good does it do to keep them? It's stupid. What do you want to go and do that for, anyway?"

"They seemed too terrible to throw away."

"So why didn't you tell any of us right from the beginning?"

"Well, you found out, didn't you?"

"How're you kids doing in there?" It was Mrs. Conrad. She popped her head in the room and smiled at them.

"We're doing okay, Mom," Blaze said, waving her away.

"Good. I'm driving your sister to dance class now, and Mrs. Alonzo's giving her a ride back. When she gets home, we'll have dinner. You're welcome to stay, Ashley."

"No, thanks, Mrs. Conrad," Ashley said. "I have to go home because of my mom."

"Okay, dear. Come and visit us again." Mrs. Conrad closed the door.

The video clicked off, and the TV screen turned to static, but neither Blaze nor Ashley moved.

"I hate being weird. I feel like I belong in a zoo most of the time," Ashley finally said.

"You aren't weird. You're special. I think you're special. I know I'm just one person, okay, but you shouldn't care what other people think. You're 'Most Unusual.' Why should you care, anyway? Let me tell you something, Ashley."

"What?"

"It never really matters what people think about you, because most people spend most of their time thinking about themselves. They're all worried about what other people think about *them*."

"All right, Blaze, how come 'Class Rebel'? We all thought you were this blue-collar kid with alcoholic parents or something because you always come to school in that black T-shirt and black jeans. Are you trying to tell me that *you* don't care what people think? You're acting like this whole other person."

"I'm not acting. Right now I *am* this other person. You can't be somebody you aren't. I'm not like the rest of my family. I'm not Quik-Whip pies and three TV rooms and Ennisclare Park. I want to be different . . . unusual, like you. What's wrong with telling people that I really live in a trailer park?"

"It's just not normal, Blaze."

"What's normal?" he asked.

"There's Heather. She's normal," Ashley answered.

"Combing your hair every three minutes is normal?"

"She *thinks* about normal things. She doesn't believe in crying; you know she can actually make herself stop crying?"

Blaze thought about that for a moment. He could believe it; Heather could probably stop herself from sweating in the Mojave Desert, too. But he couldn't cover up what he was anymore — he didn't have to do it with Tommy, why should he with his other friends?

"Ashley," Blaze explained, "that story about me — the one everybody believes — well, I guess I liked it because it helped me be more like how I see myself. I didn't have to *be* from Ennisclare Park if everyone thought I was a junkyard punk. And I don't *want* to be from here, anyway."

"But, Blaze," Ashley said, "you *are* from here. You don't have to lie to be different; you're already different. At least, I think you are."

"Ashley, if you'll just stop talking for a second, I'm going to kiss you." Blaze put his arm around Ashley.

But Blaze wasn't really thinking about kissing Ashley. It was that last note. It was written in *pink* pen. And the drawing, well, the body had *purple* blood gushing out of the place where the scissors were stuck through its heart.

Those colors clicked in his mind, and Blaze *knew* who was sending Ashley those hate notes. It was Heather Mercer. She had been doing it all the time.

Final Section

14

A week later on Saturday morning, everybody was in the Yearbook Committee room working hard. It was a cold, rainy day. It had rained all morning, and Room 228 was chilly and damp. Ashley was wearing an oversize sweater and Blaze's leather jacket.

Dolores had snuck in after Ms. Crowley had taken attendance to help them type. Dolores wasn't doing much typing. She and Heather were sitting in the corner, drawing butterflies and shooting stars on each other's eyelids.

"I'm so happy I can hardly stand it," Ashley announced.

"What for?" Blaze wasn't happy at all. He was mad. He was mad at Ms. Crowley.

"I wish we had this stuff done," Heather complained. "If we don't get this stuff done soon, we won't graduate. Worst thing about it is, we didn't even have a choice."

"Not making a choice is choosing." Blaze was up out of his chair on his feet. Prancing around the room, he flounced from one end of Room 228 to the other, mimicking Ms. Crowley's clipped eastern accent. "You four are the most uncooperative, lazy, underachieving students I have ever encountered in my short teaching career. And you're never going to amount to anything.

"And furthermore, you were put on this earth solely for the purpose of serving on the Yearbook Committee. I will not let you escape this character-building opportunity."

Dolores and Ashley clapped wildly. Terry was nodding his head. Smiling. Heather started to laugh.

After a while they went back to work. "These are good dreams for the future," Ashley announced, digging through the pile of pages in front of her. "They make me happy."

"Come on," Blaze said. "You're just happy because you finally quit rereading *Carrie*. That would make anybody happy."

"I am not! I like these guys' dreams for the future. Lester Anderson wants to be a lifeguard, Dorian Mishumi wants to be an astronaut, and Scratch Martin wants to start the first rock club in outer space. Monica Costello intends to write books for kids who are afraid they're going to get nuked. Randi Westraw wants to invent a way to tow icebergs to desert areas to prevent drought. And Anna Blume wants to become a famous singer in New York."

Terry threw his pencil down on the table, changing the subject. "You guys want to know something?"

"What?"

"It's a delicate problem."

"What is it?" Terry had Heather and Dolores's full attention. Delicate problems were their favorite kind.

"Well, what I think is this: I think it was a girl sending Ashley those hate letters."

The room went completely still. Finally Heather spoke up. "I thought we weren't going to talk about that anymore."

"I think we should decide who did it, don't you?" Terry nudged Blaze.

"I'd rather just forget it right now," Ashley said quietly.

"I agree." Blaze's voice was cold. "If Ashley doesn't want to talk about it, we should let it drop."

"I don't think I want to know, anyway," Dolores said to no one in particular.

"Let's call Mike Ross 'Most Electronically Talented.' " Blaze tried to get them off the subject.

"Yeah, okay," Terry agreed. "He's electronically talented. Like, what else can you say? He's your classic computer nerd. Dolores!" Terry pounded on the typewriter. "You and Heather can play with your eyelids some other time; get over here and type. Heather, you think of something to call Andrea Sanducci."

" 'Most Likely to Be Back Next Year,' " Blaze suggested.

"That's not fair. Make Andrea 'Most Tempestuous,' " Heather decided, sitting down beside Terry. "Who's next? We're almost done. Ashley, what's the matter?"

Ashley was curled up in her chair, looking very depressed. "Nothing."

"Are you okay?"

"No."

"What do you mean? You were the one who was so happy just a couple of minutes ago. What happened?"

"I'm not happy anymore. I'll probably be happy again, but I'm not right now."

"You've been getting really moody," Heather offered.

"Let's keep working," Blaze said. "What's wrong with you, Ashley?"

"I wish everybody would stop talking about who sent me those stupid hate letters."

"If you ask me," Heather said, fixing the barrettes in her hair, "everybody's been acting weird all year. What are we going to call Mark Huntley? We've got stuff for everybody except Mark Huntley. Can we leave him blank?" she asked with forced weariness. "From now on, if somebody doesn't turn in their stuff, I vote we leave them blank."

"We can't leave him blank. He's the only one who didn't turn something in. We have to think up something for him," Ashley said.

"Why do I get the feeling he's going to be really sorry?" Terry muttered.

"We'll think up something really nice for him," Ashley promised. "Something that's true."

"Like what?"

"I don't know. He's not one of those people

who spends a lot of time thinking ahead . . . that's the problem."

"Wait!" Everybody looked at Ashley. Ashley's face was glowing. "All Mark wants to do is go out with Francine. We'll make that his dream for the future."

"You don't think that will get him ticked off maybe just a little?"

"No way. Maybe she'll even go out with him."

"It's your funeral, kid."

"Mark won't do anything to me," Ashley smiled. "We'll tell him I did it. Mark likes me."

"He does?" There was a possessive note in Blaze's voice.

"Relax, Blaze. It's platonic."

"There's no such thing as platonic," Blaze grumbled.

"You want to bet?" Dolores put her arms around Terry and kissed him on the head. "What do you think Terry and I are?"

"They're right." Heather was sorting through piles of paper. "If they weren't platonic, they'd both be dead meat. I think platonic is a nice alternative to being dead meat, don't you, Terry?"

"You know, nothing really happened to me in all of high school before this year," Ashley said, changing the subject. "Months and months of nothing. I guess it was kind of a waste of time."

Ms. Crowley came in to dismiss them. She walked in, made sure they were all there, and gathered up the new list of tag lines.

"I suppose you're waiting for me to congratulate you," she said flatly. "Well, you haven't passed the test yet." With that, she walked out the door.

"Do you think that's supposed to mean something?" Heather asked as they listened to Ms. Crowley walk down the hall.

"Why do I get this feeling she wishes we would disappear?" Terry asked.

"I don't know; why do you?" Heather was busy packing up her bag.

"You guys!" Dolores burst out. "What're we hanging around here being depressed for? Let's go. Let's go party!"

"Where?" Heather asked practically.

It was a good question. Blaze looked at Terry, and Terry looked at Ashley; Ashley looked at Heather, and Heather looked at Dolores.

"It's *your* idea," Blaze said to Dolores. "*You* pick the place."

Dolores thought for a moment. "What about your house, Blaze?" she asked a little nervously. "We've never seen where you live — it'd be an adventure."

"You're kidding, right?" Blaze said dryly. "My house is out."

"Why?" Terry wanted to know. "I mean, there's probably nobody home, right? So we won't bother anyone. And it's just as close as anywhere else."

Blaze scowled. If Ashley had told anyone about his house, he'd have to pulp her brain. But he wasn't sure; maybe it was time that people knew where he lived. These people weren't so bad; they could even be nice sometimes. He needed time to think it over. "I guess they're probably all gone," he stalled. "Except my little brother, and he never comes out of his room. But there's really nothing to do there."

Heather sighed in exasperation. "Blaze, in case you've forgotten, there's nothing to do *here*, either."

"Besides," Dolores put in, "you don't have to provide any entertainment — we're entertaining enough all by ourselves."

Terry looked at Blaze, but he didn't offer any objections. "All right, then," he said. "It's settled. Let's go to Blaze's."

Terry pulled Heather out of her chair and dragged Dolores out the door with them. "You guys coming or what?" Heather yelled back to Blaze and Ashley.

"We're coming in a minute."

"Good. Meet you at the car."

"Yeah."

Ashley and Blaze were alone in the Yearbook Committee room. "Are you sure this is all right with you, Blaze?" she asked.

"I guess. You promised not to say anything. Did you say anything to them about where I live?"

"No, Blaze. I didn't say anything."

Blaze put his arms around Ashley and gave her his Aleutian Death Squeeze. "Good. If you did, I would have had to snap your neck."

Ashley put her face against his neck. She was saying something, but he couldn't hear it.

Her voice was muffled by his leather jacket.

"You know something, Ashley? I really, really love you."

Ashley pulled away and looked up at him. "You do?"

"Yep. And I've decided that I don't care if they all think I'm a schizo. Or a fake. They're just going to have to get to know me."

They walked outside arm in arm, bumping hips until they got to Dolores's car. Heather, Terry, and Dolores were all waiting in the car. Blaze took Ashley's hand and shoved it into his jacket pocket with his. "Look," he said, "Ashley and I'll go ahead on my bike."

"All right." Dolores nodded. "Where do you live?"

Blaze took a deep breath and told her. Dolores just about fell out of the car. "You're kidding me, right?"

"No."

"Oh. Okay, we'll meet you there."

Blaze and Ashley walked over to Blaze's cycle. Blaze unlocked it, got on, and held it steady for Ashley.

"There." Ashley climbed on, fit herself against his back, and wrapped her arms around his chest. "That wasn't so hard, was it?"

"What, are you kidding me?" Two minutes later all Blaze could hear was the roar of his motorcycle and Ashley laughing in his ear.

Blaze wished that ride could have lasted forever.

Once they got out of town, they rode down

empty roads washed by warm sunlight. Ashley was soft and wrapped around him, and Blaze suddenly wanted to spend the rest of his life just like that, riding through the world with Ashley.

When they got to Blaze's house, Dolores's car was sitting in the driveway. Blaze knew it was going to be hard showing them his house. But he had to. He hoped that they wouldn't think he was just another rich kid.

"How'd you get here so fast?" Blaze asked as he walked toward the car from his parked bike.

"You don't know how Dolores drives." Terry climbed out of the backseat and looked around. "Nice place. I mean, where's the moat?"

"This is your house, huh?" Dolores slammed her door and stood facing the house, her hands resting on her hips. "I can't believe you live here. I always thought your family must be dirt poor."

"Yeah; well, we're not."

"You'd never know it to look at you."

"Thanks. It's just I don't care how much money my parents have. It's theirs, not mine."

Blaze led them around back. He'd been right. There was nobody home but Brett. Blaze's father was still on a business trip, and it was his mother's day to drive Corin to her double art lesson. Brett was wailing on — more like murdering — his electric guitar. He was playing something that sounded like "Jimi Hendrix Meets the Beach Boys."

"Did somebody leave the stereo on?" Heather asked.

"No," said Blaze. "That's my brother. Unfortunately, he's not so easy to turn off."

They got to the kitchen door, and Blaze reassured everyone, "I'll get my brother to turn it down. He's got headphones."

Blaze opened the door, and they all walked through the kitchen.

"You got anything to eat?" Dolores asked on her way by the refrigerator.

"Sure," Blaze said. "I don't know what, though. Check it out."

Dolores opened the refrigerator. She couldn't believe what she saw. "What's with all this Tupperware? Doesn't your family ever *eat* the leftovers?"

"Sure," Blaze said. "It's just that my mom likes to keep everything *really* fresh. She thinks Tupperware's best for that."

"Okay if I try some of this?" Dolores asked, pulling out a tin of chocolate candy. Dolores ate one, gave one to Terry, then ate another. In no time, the contents of the box were severely diminished.

"How many people in your family?" Dolores asked, her mouth full of chocolate.

"Five."

"Five people in all this space?" Terry asked in amazement. "Unbelievable. It's bigger than Heather's house."

Heather didn't say anything. She just smiled, forcing back a delighted giggle. "Great carpet, Blaze." She grinned.

"Yeah. It's an Aubusson."

Heather sat down on the floor beside Dolores, took off her shoes, and rubbed her feet. "It's magnificent."

Meanwhile, Terry had gotten them all Cokes and sat down next to Heather on the floor. Dolores passed around a basket of weird-looking cookies and muffins.

"What is this?" Ashley asked, holding up a muffin.

"I don't know." Blaze looked over his shoulder. "One of my mother's new experiments. I think they're herb muffins.

"Come on," Blaze said. "Let's go into the game room and play with the VCR."

They followed him with the food into a huge game room. It had two plaid couches, a pool table, a pinball machine, and a complete video ensemble.

Blaze set up the video as the others found places on the floor, their backs against the couch, the food in front of them, watching *The Shining* on the VCR, drinking Cokes, and eating.

"This is fun, huh?" Dolores had decided.

"Well," Heather began, "it is, but I want to know one thing: Why did we all think Blaze was so poor? I mean, did you know about this house, Ashley?"

Ashley looked at her. "Yeah, but only for a little while. I guess Blaze didn't think he could trust anyone. He's really not like all of this," she added, pointing to the room's furnishings.

Heather didn't look appeased. She stared intently at Blaze until he said something.

"Look, I don't expect you to agree with me, Heather. I just don't like being identified as something I'm really not at all."

They sat there for a silent moment.

"Makes sense to me," Terry broke out cheerfully. "If I'd had this much space though, I think I'd be a whole lot happier."

"Don't be a jerk, Terry," Dolores scolded him. "Your problems don't have anything to do with your 'space.'"

"I can't believe this year is practically over already. This is not how I was expecting to spend my senior year, believe me. You know," Ashley said, leaning against Blaze's shoulder, "maybe my mother was right. You've got to hang around for the surprises."

"Like, for instance, this house," Dolores said, teasing.

"Come on, Dolores," Terry pleaded.

"It's just that, well, I heard you were always giving Heather this grief, Blaze, because she's this really rich kid. And look where you live."

"I know," Blaze confessed. "But that's the difference between Heather and me: She *likes* being rich."

"Don't *you*?" Heather snapped. "This is, after all, a very nice place."

"I don't own it and never will," Blaze said quietly.

Heather considered this silently, while Ashley and the others got distracted by the movie on the VCR. Soon they had all settled in to watch *The Shining* in earnest.

"This doesn't look like real life at all," Ashley said. "It's great. But I still think it's kind of artsy, no offense."

"It isn't supposed to look like real life." Heather handed Terry a green muffin. "It's the movies."

"Yeah. But it's scary, anyway. Don't you think it's scary?" Ashley asked, her eyes wide open.

They were halfway through the scary part, when all of a sudden, they were practically deafened by an electric guitar cranking full-blown in the middle of "In a Gadda da Vida."

"What's that!" Dolores screamed. "I think I'm in love."

"You're not in love, trust me," Blaze corrected. "That's my brother again."

"We've *heard* so much about him, let's *meet* him now. Bring him out here, and introduce me! 'In a Gaddada Vida!' I'm like, blissed out, okay?" Dolores was seriously affected by Brett's treatment of the song.

"Dolores, my brother's only twelve years old."

Dolores leaned back on the couch and spread her arms out in an attempt to soak up every note Brett managed to squeeze out of his guitar. "Oh, yeah? Well, hey, what's ten years? I can wait."

Later that night after they'd all gone home, Blaze went downstairs to the basement and opened the freezer. Blaze was determined to get revenge on Heather for terrorizing Ashley. He'd thought it all out. The perfect revenge. It had taken him practically all night. He dug through frozen vegetables and minute steaks and family-size packages of bologna until he got to the bottom. The sea bass his father had caught last summer was still in the freezer, solidly stuck to the bottom in a thick block of blue ice. Blaze walked across the room to the tool chest and pulled out a long screwdriver. Then he went back to the freezer and began chipping out the fish. He only hit the fish once, behind its gills. He investigated the damage and figured it would be okay.

After he dug the fish out completely, he put the loose chips back in the freezer along with all the other food he'd taken out. He took the fish upstairs. It was really heavy.

Blaze practically destroyed his closet trying to find a box big enough to put the fish in. He went down the hall to his parents' room and searched his mother's closet until he found a dress box. It was perfect. It was full of pink tissue paper. Blaze went back to his room, put the box on the bed, and wrapped up the fish in the tissue paper.

Then he wrapped the whole box in brown paper and slapped about ten dollars of stamps on it, which he also borrowed from his mother's room. Finally he wrote Heather Mercer's address on it in waterproof black magic marker.

Blaze took a shower and went to bed smiling. He'd mail the present tomorrow. Heather would know from his handwriting that he was on to her. If she was smart, which Blaze suspected she was, she'd quit sending Ashley hate mail.

It was perfect. Tomorrow was Friday. It would take an entire weekend to get to the Mercers'.

15

A week later Heather, Terry, Blaze, and Ashley were back in Room 228. They were getting down to the wire. Ms. Crowley expected them to turn in their tag lines in exactly two hours and had already made it clear that their current stack of ripped typewritten pages and unreadable handwritten scribblings on the backs of cigarette packs, candy bar wrappers, and shopping bags, would not be acceptable. She wanted a little more organization. She wanted a lot more dedication. Ms. Crowley, they all decided, wanted them to sweat blood.

"I am not typing all those pages myself!" Heather exploded. "It's ruining my nails." Heather had only typed two pages. Her shoulders hurt from hunching over the typewriter in what Heather was convinced was an unattractive posture. She wasn't about to sacrifice her award-winning beauty to hunt and peck — or to the Yearbook Committee.

"Well, it's your typewriter," Blaze pointed out. "And, anyway, I can't type."

"That's what guys always say," Heather complained. " 'I can't type,' " she mimicked Blaze's laid-back voice. "Like typing's *so* hard. All you do is put your finger on the letter and push. I guess maybe even *you* can handle that."

Blaze scowled, but Ashley, coming up behind both of them and putting her hands on Blaze's shoulders, laughed. The girl was full of surprises these days, Heather thought. She had decided lately — ever since the dead fish had arrived in the Bloomingdale's box at her front door — that maybe Ashley had hidden depths. Maybe she shouldn't have tried so hard to freak Ashley out. Maybe Ashley didn't really deserve all that torment.

Heather, who prided herself on being able to read people, could kick herself for never once guessing that Ashley would have had the imagination and guts to pull off her revenge. Not only that, but Ashley had somehow penetrated Heather's defenses: She was actually feeling a little guilty about writing those notes.

Maybe, Heather decided, Ashley wasn't as vague as she looked. Maybe the vague routine was all an act like Heather's own dumb-blonde routine. Maybe secretly Ashley was trying to make Heather feel guilty by acting so ignorant. Heather thought then and there she and Ashley probably had more in common than she'd ever dreamed in her worst nightmares: Ashley could be sly, too.

Terry leaned over Heather's shoulder and read the typed list of tag lines aloud. Terry smelled like he had smeared Essence of Old

Irish Bog all over himself. Heather had tried to take him shopping for cologne, but Terry's taste was in the gutter.

"Hey, this is great stuff," Terry read. "Danny Defalco, 'Most Likely to Wear Polyester'; Jennifer Donovan, 'Best Candidate for an Obscure Eastern Religious Group.'"

"What does this say?" Heather asked, squinting at Blaze's handwriting in the margin of an article entitled "Helpful Cuisinart Cooking Tips" by Eileen Conrad.

Blaze, standing three-deep behind Heather, looked over Terry's shoulder to see over Heather's shoulder.

"That's Janet Melberhardt. 'Most Stuck-Up.'"

Ashley had gone back to her place from across the table where she was making her own list, printing it out in her small, precise script. Her fingers were covered with ink from where her pen leaked down her hand. She had smudges on her nose. She was trying to concentrate despite the noise coming from Heather's side of the table.

Blaze suddenly thought Ashley looked very beautiful. More beautiful than Heather, with her perfect makeup job and her perfect clothes and her perfect face. Heather was so perfect, she might as well be immortalized in plastic for future generations.

"You can't say that," Ashley protested.

"I can't say 'Stuck-Up'? Why not? All right, 'Most Arrogant.'"

"But she's not arrogant. Janet's just shy. She's okay."

"Shy?" Blaze and Terry chorused.

Terry shook his head. "Hey, I smiled at that girl for three weeks running, and she wouldn't give me the time of day. That's not shy. That's brain-dead."

"Don't sweat it, Wallace; she's immune." Blaze sat down on the worktable. "High school guys aren't good enough for Ms. Orthodontically Correct Melberhardt," Blaze told Terry. "She's got some guy picking her up after school in a BMW."

"You've objected to nearly every tag anybody has come up with, Ashley," protested Heather. "Do you want to just do this yourself? I mean, I don't even know why we bother sitting in the same room with you."

"You guys," Ashley said, ignoring Heather, "Janet's mother is in the hospital. Would you care about some guy like Terry chatting you up in the halls if your mother had cancer? The guy in the BMW is her brother; he picks her up after school to go over to the hospital. She's never been nice to me, either, but it's not fair to give her a rotten tag when her life is so rotten already."

"So, what do *you* suggest?" Blaze demanded. Blaze was embarrassed. Being embarrassed made him mad.

"It's like I keep saying!" Ashley was getting carried away. "I can't believe how stupid this whole tag line idea is. There's more to John

Abisimira than his great arms, or like it's Danny Defalco's fault that he's got ugly polyester clothes when everybody knows his dad has been out of work for two years, or . . . oh, forget it. You've heard all this before."

"We don't have enough time to debate moral issues," Heather shot out before she could stop herself. "If you have a problem with the way society works, go find yourself a cause. In the meantime, we all have about two seconds to pull this whole thing together, guys. In case you haven't noticed, it's panic time." Heather began to chew on a manicured hot-pink fingernail. Then she looked at her finger as she realized what she was doing: ruining a perfect nail. She recoiled from her hand in horror. She hadn't chewed her nails since she was a fat preadolescent. She thought long and hard for a minute. "On the other hand. . . ."

Ashley looked like she was going to fall out of her chair. "You're agreeing with me?"

"Well, don't expect it to become a habit or anything. But I'm thinking, you could be right. Maybe there's more to me than being 'Most Beautiful.' There's certainly more to *you*, Blaze Conrad, than 'Class Rebel,' " Heather added, turning toward Blaze. "Maybe being beautiful is just the first thing you notice about me, but I'm really . . . oh, 'Most Likely to Succeed' or something," she suggested casually. "And maybe," she went on, glaring at Blaze, who was choking with laughter, "*Ashley is right*. We shouldn't be labeling people by just what's on the surface or what we think we know about them — "

"Spare me, Heather," Blaze interrupted. "Did you think up all those big words by yourself?"

"Stop it, Blaze," Ashley ordered. "Heather got the point; why can't you?"

"Sorry." Lately Blaze seemed to be apologizing a lot.

"You are forgiven," Heather said imperiously. She pulled a nail file out of her bag and smoothed the ragged end of her bitten nail.

"I don't know," Blaze said to Heather. "I guess it makes sense. It's just I'm in shock that anything you say makes sense."

"Why didn't it make sense when *I* first brought it up? Back when we started all this?" Ashley wanted to know.

"You were too vague, Ashley. Like I've been trying to tell you. You have to stick up for your opinions; you can't wait around for someone like Heather to come along and stick up *for* you. Be decisive for a change."

"Yeah, but what does all this mean in real terms?" Terry asked impatiently. "That we tell Crowley we think the whole idea is a crock and bag this Yearbook Committee business? What if she doesn't buy it?"

"She won't buy it," Heather said glumly, turning back to the typewriter. "You know Crowley. Let's just get this junk finished, okay, boys and girls? I want to get down to the mall before it closes. I'll type one more page, and then someone else has to take over."

Ashley crossed the room and pulled the sheet of paper out of the typewriter. She crumpled it into a ball and threw it against the wall.

"Hey," Heather protested. "I just finished that page. What are you doing?"

Ashley looked at Blaze. Blaze was standing in the middle of the room. A slow smile was spreading across his face.

"I'm being decisive," Ashley informed them all.

Ashley was far from decisive when Ms. Crowley walked in the door at the end of the morning, however. Ms. Crowley picked up the typewritten pages, paper-clipped at the top with a banana paper clip. "Is this some kind of joke?" she asked, frowning. "Is this ... list ... all you intend to turn in to me?"

"No," Blaze corrected, "We also have a list of Future Dreams and Aspirations that we collected from all the seniors." Blaze pushed a navy folder across the worktable.

Ms. Crowley glanced briefly through the rather hefty folder. Then she shifted her attention back to the pages in her hand.

She took a deep breath and looked around the room. Her eyes glinted like ice chips in a glacier. "Yes, but the *assignment* was to vote on 'Most Likely' tags for the school yearbook. Do you mean to tell me that this" — she waved the pages in the air in front of them — "was all the four of you could come up with? In all these days of work?"

Nobody said a word.

This was serious. Maybe one of the most

serious things that had ever happened to them. "I must say I'm very disappointed in you. In all of you. As your parents will be, I daresay, when you explain why you are not graduating with your class. Did you think that was an idle threat?"

Ms. Crowley shook her head and frowned some more to emphasize just how disappointed she was. Terry noticed she was wearing the putty-colored shirt again. Somebody should make her burn that shirt, Terry thought.

Terry glanced anxiously at Ashley. She was just looking at her desk again. Changing the Yearbook had been her idea; if she didn't pull this off, they were all going to suffer. She had to say something. Preferably soon. If she didn't, Terry had something more horrible than hate notes in store for Ashley. That is, unless his parents murdered him for not graduating first.

Blaze slouched lower in his chair, cleaning his fingernails with his Swiss Army knife. His hair fell over his eyes, as if it could cover him, make him invisible. Well, Blaze decided, he could always work at the Sunoco station next year.

Ms. Crowley droned on about how they had been given a chance but had blown her trust by being irresponsible.

". . . This hardly counts as fulfilling your obligation to the school or me. Did you really expect the Yearbook adviser to approve these? You really thought these would appear in print?" She looked at the pages and read at random. "'Most Likely to Be Kidnapped by

Canadian Terrorists.' 'Most Likely to Mate with an Extraterrestrial.' 'Most Likley to Be Reincarnated as an Opossum.' . . . Is this your idea of humor? These are . . . idiotic." She threw the pages down in disgust.

"Ashley . . ." Heather murmured. There was a plea in her voice.

Blaze looked up. He was waiting for Ashley, too. He got her started with a kick, and he kicked her *hard*.

Ashley sat up and looked around, as if waking from a trance. "That's because the whole idea is idiotic," she said loudly. She bit her lip remembering that the whole idea had been Ms. Crowley's. "I mean . . ." she tried to explain.

"We decided it was silly to label people like this," Heather spoke up.

Ashley glanced toward Heather uncertainly. Heather wasn't looking at her. She was carefully pressing her hands on the tabletop. "Yeah," Ashley ventured. "We decided that what people thought about *themselves* was more important than what *we* thought about them. That's why we collected everybody's dreams and fantasies in the first place. They tell you more about the kids in the senior class than any dumb tags the four of us could come up with."

"That's right," Terry agreed. "I mean, *I* don't really want to be known as 'Class Flirt'; why would anyone else?"

But Ms. Crowley was still frowning. She picked up the blue folder. "This is all very nice," she said. "But we still have a problem here. You didn't fulfill the assignment."

"Yes, we did," Terry put in. He, for one, was fighting for his life. "We gave everybody a tag. You may think they don't fulfill the assignment, but we've tried to be honest. They're more responsible than the tag lines kids hand out every year."

"And more harmless," Blaze added, snapping the Swiss Army blade shut. "Nobody's going to get hurt by these. They're funny, and they're true. Did you know that last year they actually voted one poor guy 'Worst Complexion'?"

"Anyway," Ashley pointed out logically, "wasn't the whole point of this assignment to get us to work together, seeing as we're all kind of noninvolved types? To get us to do something to show some initiative and some school spirit? Well, we have. And we got to know one another in the process. I think we even got to like one another. So it's not fair for you to say we haven't done our job just because you don't like the way we tried to do it best. We all took a vote, and we did it as a team. Isn't that what you wanted?"

Ms. Crowley looked through the blue folder. Her expression grew thoughtful as she stopped skimming and began to read in earnest.

The four Yearbook Committee members waited silently. They acted nonchalant — as if graduation didn't depend on her response or as if they didn't care whether they graduated at all.

Another year in this crummy hole, Heather thought. I'll die, she decided desperately as she stared into her compact mirror trying to dig a flake of mascara out of the corner of her eye. Her entire eye was beginning to tear. Another year here? . . . Chauncey, well, Chauncey will get a real laugh and a half out of this one.

Ashley's heart was beating fast. She wished she didn't care. She wished she could just let her thoughts drift into the ozone, where nothing was real and nothing really mattered. But it was scaring her to discover how much she really *did* care. What if everybody failed because of her?

Blaze didn't care if he failed or not. If he was stuck back in school another year, that was the breaks. Being a forest ranger could wait. But Ashley wouldn't graduate, either. She wouldn't go for that. And even though he was beginning to think that anywhere Ashley was was okay by him, Blaze knew they had to fight for their principles.

Terry had it the worst. He couldn't stand it anymore. It was like being at home waiting for his parents to make a decision, waiting to see if they were going to be calm or if they were going to explode. It was like being a little kid again, his life dependent on someone else's mood and whim. He jumped up and began to pace rapidly back and forth, walking off his energy. Ms. Crowley looked up from the blue folder abruptly, startled.

"This is actually . . . well, quite good," she said. She clipped the pages of Future Dreams and Aspirations together and tucked them into her briefcase. For some reason, she was still frowning. "Terry, sit down. Relax. You have a reprieve. I'll speak to Mr. Langley about accepting this as well as the tag lines we can manage to salvage. And I will admit that your work has a certain . . . egalitarian spirit." She snapped the briefcase shut. "But the four of you will have to bear the responsibility for your decision — just as in the real world. Your classmates will be expecting to see tag lines in the yearbook, as usual, when they are handed out at the Yearbook Dance. I expect all four of you to be there. It's your party. You can cry if you want to, but you're the ones who will have to deal with the consequences."

"I never go to dances," Blaze said quickly.

Ms. Crowley smiled sweetly at him as she left the room. "You do now."

"Terrific," Blaze muttered. "Just terrific. Does this never end?"

"Come on, Blaze," Heather said, picturing herself in the little red Betsey Johnson minidress her mother hated, that she'd bought especially for the dance. "I bet it will be fun."

"*Fun?*" Ashley and Blaze looked at each other in horror.

16

It was not fun. Not at all. It was probably the worst night of Heather's life.

First her mother, as predicted, had a fit about the dress. It was too short. It was too tight. It made her look cheap. It would give boys ideas. As if boys didn't have enough ideas of their own already. What nice girl would want to be seen in a red dress that short with black lace tights and black high heels?

Every girl who's ever watched MTV, Mother. It was no good explaining to her mother that there'd be plenty of "nice girls" at the dance looking even cheaper.

Then, to top off the whole argument, her mother had suggested she run upstairs to see if she couldn't find "some little old thing of Chauncey's." As if she'd ever be caught dead in old Chauncey's hand-me-downs. They were collecting dust under her bed, where they belonged.

When Terry's car arrived, she ran out the door. Well, staggered, actually. The heels on her shoes were awfully high. She could still hear her mother's voice as she got into the car, slammed the door, and ordered Terry to go.

She'd been so angry about the whole scene that they were halfway to school before she realized that Terry was upset himself — pale, silent, his knuckles white where he was clenching the steering wheel.

"It's nothing," he said when she asked him what was wrong. "Just my folks. . . . Aw, forget it. You look great tonight, Heather; you really do."

Heather, uncharacteristically, barely noticed the compliment, and forgot all about the argument with her mother. She'd never seen Terry look so upset — not since the time she'd yelled at him about the awful perfume. She wished she knew what to say to him. She smoothed back her hair, checked her face in her compact, and squeezed Terry's knee, in what she hoped was a comforting gesture. She did look drop-dead gorgeous tonight. That ought to cheer Terry up.

At the dance, though, things went from bad to worse.

First of all, Janet Melberhardt was wearing a dress exactly like hers — and Janet's figure was stupendous.

Yearbooks were being handed out at the door by the members of the Student Council. All the seniors were eagerly paging through the red and black bound books, looking for themselves and their friends, anxious to see who had been voted what, and what had been said about them. It came as a shock when they found only four pages of tag lines. The other twenty pages had

Future Dreams and Aspirations printed beneath the airbrushed studio portraits. There was, for instance, no "Most Popular," no "Most Athletic," and no "Most Likely to Succeed."

Ashley and Blaze were nowhere to be seen. Terry was standing on the side. For once in his life he wasn't surrounded by girls. No one was talking to him. He was holding his yearbook and fiddling with a white corsage he'd picked up from the floor.

Heather, standing in the middle of the dance floor, was looking forward to being the center of attention, to giving out the carefully worded explanations she and Ashley had worked out. But nobody wanted to hear her explanations. She felt like Terry looked — used and abandoned.

"You promised me I'd be 'Most Glamorous,'" Stella Catwaller hissed in Heather's ear. Stella had been Heather's best friend once. Now Stella made it absolutely clear that she would refuse to speak to Heather ever again.

"You told me I would be 'Most School-Spirited,'" Johnny Weiss complained. "I already put it on my application to Ohio State."

"There's always a 'Most Theatrical' every year," Dana Hildebrant told Heather. "What do you mean you didn't vote for a 'Most Theatrical' this year?"

Life went on like that for a while — petulant kids complaining about their absent tag lines.

Heather was grateful when the band began to play. They were a local band, very loud and not very good, but they saved her from having to listen to more threats and complaints. She went over to Terry and clutched his hand as they threaded through the crowd. He smiled at people as they passed, but his hand was cold. She decided then and there she didn't want ever to let it go.

The lights of the gym had been dimmed, except for the floodlights over the basketball scoreboard and blinking colored Christmas lights strung along the bleachers — the pep squad's attempt to make the gym look like their idea of a rock club. In the dark and press of the bodies, Heather lost Terry. As she searched the crowd for him, peering over shoulders and around gyrating bodies, she caught a glimpse of Janet Melberhardt in her identical red minidress — and Terry laughing down at her, saying something with his head close to her ear.

Outside, in the parking lot, Blaze and Ashley were driving up on Blaze's bike. The parking lot was crammed with cars and crowds of students, mostly boys. They were clustered in groups, yelling at one another, sitting on car hoods, shoving one another into moving vehicles.

The Night Riders took up one whole corner of the parking lot, leaning against their cars with their arms crossed over their chests. All of the Night Riders were scowling.

"I don't want to go inside," Ashley said, climbing down from Blaze's bike.

"Neither do I."

"Let's go somewhere else," Ashley pleaded.

"Later." Blaze put his arm around Ashley,

and they walked toward the auditorium, through the catcalls of the Night Riders.

On their way through the door, Simon Esterhazy shoved a yearbook into Blaze's stomach.

"Thanks."

"Where's Terry and Heather?" Ashley asked, peering into the packed gym.

"Good luck trying to find them," Blaze said. "It's like an insect swarm in here."

That's when Ms. Crowley found them. Ms. Crowley was wearing some kind of dress that came down to the middle of her calves and covered her entire body. In the dim light, the dress looked like a muddy army tent. She was waving a list. Terry was trailing unhappily behind her. "Have any of you seen Heather Mercer?" she demanded.

No one had.

"She was here a minute ago," Terry finally stated in a flat voice.

"It's eight o'clock," Ms. Crowley informed them. And you know what that means, don't you?"

The three of them stared at one another. They knew what that meant. It meant they had to climb up onto the stage with the band and speak into the microphone. They had to read out the names and Future Dreams and Aspirations for the solo dances.

"Go on." Ms. Crowley gave Ashley, who was standing next to her, a little push. "The three of you will have to get on up there. In the meantime, I'll go find Heather."

"Check the bathroom," Terry advised. "She's probably fixing her makeup."

The sooner they got it over with, the better. The three of them circled through the moving bodies on the dance floor and climbed up the side of the stage. Ashley was so nervous she almost fell.

The band looked up at them in surprise. The bass player missed a beat and threw off the group momentarily.

"What're you doing up here?" the lead singer hissed.

Terry waved the page of Future Dreams and Aspirations in front of the lead singer's face. "We're here to deejay the solos. You know, spotlight and all?"

"All three of you?" The lead singer stumbled over the mike and caught it seconds before it crashed to the floor.

"Afraid so," Terry said.

"There's no room up here," the lead singer complained.

Blaze gave the lead singer a drop-dead stare, and the singer shut up.

Finally the song ended in a screech of feedback. Terry adjusted the microphone, and with Ashley standing miserably behind him and Blaze holding the band at bay, he turned on the charm.

"Good evening, everybody. The other members of the Yearbook Committee and I would like to welcome you to the annual Prescott High Yearbook Dance. . . ."

There were boos and hisses from the crowd.

". . . As you've no doubt already noticed, the yearbook has been set up a little differently this year. . . ."

More boos and hisses.

"But the more things change, the more they stay the same. . . ."

Blaze looked over at Ashley and rolled his eyes.

". . . We have kept the tradition of spotlight solos, so, if you're all ready, we'll begin." Terry turned to the band leader. "Play something," he prompted.

"Like what?"

"I don't know, something slow."

The band launched into their own scratchy rendition of "Don't Stop the Dance."

"John Abisimira," Terry read, clearing his throat nervously. "John's dream for the future is to develop a low-cost, high protein substance that will virtually end world hunger."

The spotlight swept the gymnasium floor and picked out John Abisimira, who was blushing madly. He led Ginny Logan onto the dance floor. Terry riffled through his notes. "John is dancing with Ginny Logan," he announced. "Ginny wants to be the fastest driver in America."

People on the dance floor who knew Ginny Logan's driving habits began to laugh good-naturedly and applauded.

Terry moved on, an uncertain smile across his face. "Scratch Martin wants to start the first rock club on the moon."

Scratch was beaming. He lead Susan Matsumori out onto the dance floor.

Terry grinned as the spotlight caught the couple in momentary stardom. "Susan Matsumori wants to devote her life to searching for the most perfect sound system."

Emil Ruiz jumped out onto the dance floor with Kate DeLuca. The spotlight picked them up instantly, and they both laughed as Terry read out their hopes for the future. Emil wanted to be elected to Congress on a kindness-to-alien-life-forms platform, and Kate wanted to study air recycling.

One by one, Terry moved down the list. It didn't take nearly as long as he'd thought. He even worked in Ashley and Blaze, who danced together for about a minute before disappearing out of the spotlight, which had picked them up on the stage. Soon the gym was full of dancing students, momentarily famous for whatever they had chosen as their future goals. It seemed they'd forgotten all about the tag lines and were ready to make the *new* yearbook a yearly institution. They were happy, dreaming of what could be ahead of them.

When Terry was finished announcing, he was wringing wet and smiling. Not only had they done the assignment, they were a success! Everyone burst out clapping, and the band launched into a fast dance as Terry, Ashley, and Blaze slipped off the stage. Although they tried to stay together, as soon as they hit the dance floor, the dancers separated them from one another.

"Terry!" Lisa Donnelly threw her arms around his neck and kissed him on the mouth.

"I love you. You were great." Terry held Lisa Donnelly in his arms in surprise. Oh, no, he thought. I was sure I was done with Lisa Donnelly for good.

In the meantime, Ms. Crowley had dragged Heather from the ladies' room, and Heather had stood at the back of the auditorium while Terry deejayed the solo spots. She could hardly wait for him to get finished. She decided that, then and there, she loved Terry as she had never loved anyone in her entire life. She watched him leave the stage and pushed her way through the dancers just in time to see him kissing Lisa Donnelly. Heather was mortified. First Janet Melberhardt, now Lisa. Heather turned her back on them and shoved her way through to the exit door.

She slipped through the doorway and into a dark hall. She heard someone call her name. It was one of the Night Riders, who was probably mad that he hadn't been named "Most Vicious." She ducked into a stairwell and fled down the stairs, her high heels sliding dangerously on the Formica tiles. There was only one place that was safe from all these people.

Ashley looked up in surprise as Heather switched on the light in Room 228.

"What are *you* doing in here?" she asked Ashley. "Why are you sitting here?"

Ashley looked ridiculous. Oh, the dress was all right, if you liked the vintage clothing sort of thing. But did she have to ruin it with high-topped sneakers beneath the full skirt and lace petticoat?

"What are *you* doing here?" Ashley asked in return. "Where were you during the spotlight dances? Everyone was actually having a great time. I thought you'd be there."

"I was there," Heather said vaguely.

"I hate dances," Ashley said simply. "I never know who to look at or where to put my hands."

"I hate them, too."

"Since when?"

"Since now."

Heather threw herself down on a chair and felt her patterned stocking run. She no longer cared. She kicked off her shoes and massaged the kinks in her feet.

"I don't get it," she confessed. "Terry and I came here together. One minute in the public eye and he forgets all about me."

"What happened?" Ashley asked.

"I saw him with Lisa Donnelly. They were having a very intimate moment. I can't believe I was such an idiot." Heather looked at Ashley and was surprised to see genuine sympathy in Ashley's eyes.

"You're not used to that, are you?" Ashley asked.

"Well, no. Boys have always liked me . . . wanted me to go out with them. . . ."

"People have always hated me."

"They don't hate you," Heather said. "They just think you're a little weird."

"Somebody hates me. Somebody hated me enough to write all those vile letters."

Heather shifted uncomfortably in her seat. Ashley had already gotten her revenge with the rotten fish. Why was she rubbing it in? Did she want Heather to grovel? "Sometimes people just do dumb things, you know? I mean, I wouldn't take it personally if I were you."

"You wouldn't take hate mail addressed to you and about you *personally*?" Ashley couldn't believe it. She started to laugh. "Heather, maybe you're right. It's all pretty juvenile when you think about it. . . ."

Heather squirmed again. "Yeah. Well, I'm sorry, okay? Can't we just stop this; I mean, I know and you know, and I know you know."

"What?" Ashley was confounded.

"Ashley, I know you sent me that dead fish in the mail. You got your revenge and, really, I'm actually sorry about it now."

"This is too much," Ashley mumbled. "Are you telling me that you know *I* sent you a dead fish? 'Cause if you are, we need to talk. Like maybe for a long time."

Heather was confused now, too. She couldn't understand why Ashley wouldn't just get mad or forgive her or something. "Look, Ashley, I've learned a lot during this whole yearbook thing, and I'm willing to say that I was wrong about you. And maybe about what I did."

Ashley just sat there, staring at Heather. After a long moment her mouth dropped open. "*You* sent me those notes? I can't believe it. It was you all the time? I think I'm going to puke."

Ashley put her chin in her hands and looked at her high tops. "And I thought we'd gotten over being enemies," she said quietly.

"I hope we have," Heather said. She realized that it was going to be harder to clear up this mess than she'd thought. Ashley was being stubborn. "I'm sorry."

"Well," Ashley said, sitting up straight, "it doesn't matter anymore, I guess. Only, I never even suspected *you*. There were others I thought . . . but I can't imagine why you'd bother."

"I suppose it's because I was jealous of you. You were saying what you thought about the yearbook, and I didn't even give it one thought beyond what was expected. I was jealous of the attention you were getting." Heather breathed a sigh of relief. She felt good, unburdened.

"And you thought I knew you'd sent the notes? Amazing." Ashley was regaining her composure. She actually felt better now, knowing the culprit had only been Heather. After all, it could be worse: it could've been Pudgy Varley and the Night Riders. "It doesn't matter anymore, Heather. Really. I'm impressed that you admitted it."

Heather was wondering if she had admitted it, or if Ashley had really just tricked her into saying something, when they heard Terry's voice down the hall.

"Hey, what's going on in here?" Terry said accusingly, coming in the door with Dolores in tow, the two of them dragging Blaze between them. "Are you having fun without us?"

"Look who we found cowering behind the bleachers!" Dolores said, laughing. Dolores was all vamped out in a Blister Kings T-shirt, leather jacket, and jeans. "He was white as a ghost. And trembling."

"I *really* hate dances," Blaze muttered. "Crowd claustrophobia. I think I'm gonna break out in hives."

"You should have brought your little brother," Dolores complained. "I'll bet *he* knows how to dance!"

"Sure he does," Blaze said, recovering his color and his sneer. "But it's past his bedtime."

He sat down beside Ashley. "So, this is where you've been hiding?"

"Man, I don't blame you," Terry said.

"Oh, I don't know," Heather said sarcastically. "It looked like Janet Melberhardt and her body, not to mention Lisa Donnelly, were making you feel like the star of the show."

"Can I help it if I looked up and you were gone? What am I supposed to do, never talk to another female in the universe?"

Heather opened her mouth to snap back at Terry. Then she shut it. She decided she could live without always being the center of attention. Just look at Ashley, she told herself.

"No. That's not what I meant," Heather apologized. "I don't want to fight tonight, Terry, okay?"

Terry got a funny look on his face. He came over and sat on the worktable beside her. "No, let's never *ever* fight."

"Fat chance," Dolores said cheerfully, sending Blaze and Ashley into hysterics.

"I can survive a while longer at home with

all the fighting," Terry went on, "but when I'm with my friends . . ." — he stopped and looked around the room — ". . . when I'm with my friends, I can't stand it. I guess I just want you all to like me, and to get along."

Blaze turned to Ashley. "What do you say we hang around with the rest of these social rejects for a while longer, then take my bike and go for a nice long ride — maybe up past the hills?"

Ashley smiled and nodded. "But I'm not exactly dressed for it," she warned, fingering the hem of her lace petticoat.

"Sure you are," Blaze encouraged. "You can wear my jacket. By the way, those are great sneaks." He squeezed her hand where it rested beside him and stood up.

Heather smirked. She couldn't stop herself. "Well, you always were 'Most Unusual,' Ashley." Then she added with a shrug, " 'Course, on you, it looks good."

"Okay, Wallace," Blaze said. "Meet you back at my house in twenty."

Terry grinned and pulled Heather and Dolores out into the hall with him as Blaze and Ashley followed a close second.

"Terry," Heather was complaining, "you're stretching my dress."

Terry winked at Dolores.

"And you really are the biggest flirt. Probably the biggest flirt in the whole world, forget the high school," Heather decided.

Terry stopped dead in his tracks, pulled Heather into his arms, and gave her a long kiss.

"Did I ever tell you I think you're the most beautiful?" he whispered.

"What?" Dolores burst out, "I thought you said Jello Biafra was 'Most Beautiful.'" She laughed to herself.

"No, silly, he's 'Most Sensitive,'" Ashley chuckled. "But come on, let's move it."

"Yeah," Blaze bellowed. "Move it. We've got adventures out there."

Then together they all walked out of the school into the night.

point™
Pass the word!

Order these NEW titles chosen with you in mind!

- ☐ 33556-1   **THE BET** by Ann Reit $2.25 U.S./$2.95 CAN.
- ☐ 40326-5   **BLIND DATE** by R.L. Stine $2.25 U.S./$2.95 CAN.
- ☐ 40116-5   **DISCONTINUED** by Julian F. Thompson $2.75 U.S./$3.50 CAN.
- ☐ 40251-X   **DON'T CARE HIGH** by Gordon Korman $2.50 U.S./$3.50 CAN.
- ☐ 33551-0   **HAPPILY EVER AFTER** by Hila Colman $2.25 U.S./$2.95 CAN.
- ☐ 33579-0   **HIGH SCHOOL REUNION** by Carol Stanley $2.25 U.S./$2.95 CAN.
- ☐ 40292-7   **THE KARATE KID: PART II** by B.B. Hiller $2.50 U.S./$2.95 CAN.
- ☐ 40156-4   **SATURDAY NIGHT** by Caroline B. Cooney $2.50 U.S./$3.50 CAN.
- ☐ 33926-5   **SEVEN DAYS TO A BRAND-NEW ME** by Ellen Conford $2.25 U.S./$2.95 CAN.
- ☐ 32924-3   **THIS STRANGE NEW FEELING** by Julius Lester $2.25 U.S./$2.95 CAN.
- ☐ 32923-5   **TO BE A SLAVE** by Julius Lester $2.25 U.S./$2.95 CAN.
- ☐ 33637-1   **WEEKEND** by Christopher Pike $2.25 U.S./$2.95 CAN.

Scholastic Inc.
P.O. Box 7502, 2932 East McCarty Street, Jefferson City, MO 65102

Please send me the books I have checked above. I am enclosing $_____ (please add $1.00 to cover shipping and handling). Send check or money order—no cash or C.O.D.'s please.

Name_____

Address_____

City_____ State/Zip_____
Please allow four to six weeks for delivery. Offer good in U.S.A. only. Sorry, mail order not available to residents of Canada.

POI861